UNDERNEATH
the C GREEN
anopy

DEWEY LEE SIMMS

ISBN 978-1-64471-237-5 (Paperback)
ISBN 978-1-64471-238-2 (Digital)

Covenant Books, Inc.
11661 Hwy 707
Murrells Inlet, SC 29576
www.covenantbooks.com

1

CHAPTER

Start of the Stone Family Legacy

It was days with the temperature hovering around ninety-two to ninety-six degrees in July 1932. One can sense the grandeur of this old white oak farm located on route 103 with the White Oak Road as a sideroad running into Route 103. The farmhouse is a big beautiful house with several White Oak trees surrounding the house. These trees provided much shade for the yard and for the house on these very hot summer days.

The house is a large two-story brick structure that gives the appearance of a southern plantation that would make most folks envious even though it was built back in the early 1800s. Along both sides of the White Oak Road a planting of many species of trees, and some are brought down from the Appalachian Mountains. The very thick planting of trees was a concatenate row of trees that gives some privacy to the house and yard.

The house is positioned between the two roads, and of course, the main highway is route 103 that runs east and west from Lincolnton to Concord, North Carolina. The side road is in the honor of the white oak farm that runs north and south, and this is where all the canopy of trees is planted. The canopy of trees is so thick that it is hard for sunlight to penetrate; leaving a lot of moisture on the lower limbs; causing moss to grow which is unusual for this part of the country. They offered much canopy to the road and part of the yard. It's most picturesque looking down the road that seemed almost endless with the canopy of beauty.

Stories have been told over the years about the house and how it was built for the Stone family, and it is still owned and operated by the fourth generation and now going into the fifth generation. The Stone family over the course of years has maintained their high-level of reputation and integrity. Not many families find themselves in the good graces of the community the way this family has for four generations.

The farm has some 4,300 acres, and much of the land has been cleared over the years for crops and for livestock. It was reported at one time they had some three hundred heads of cattle and much of it was for milking. Back in the very late 1700s, when the farm was first getting started, much of the work hands were slaves; so one could call the farm a plantation after all. There is no record of how many slave families was part of the farm back in the early 1800s and up to the Civil War period.

White Oak Farm House
In Rural Lincoln County, North Carolina

Now things may be changing a bit because of a pretty little eighteen-year-old daughter named Mary Elizabeth Stone, but most people just call her Lily, and the name just fits her personality. Every year, as the lilies were blooming, Mary Elizabeth as a small child loved to play in the lily garden. She would spend countless hours in the flower bed playing. So everyone started to call her "Lily" for short, and as she grew older the name stayed with her.

She is full of energy and is always on the move, always warm, and sweet to each person that she encounters no matter how old or young they are. It makes a person wonder if some of the younger men take her friendliness as flirting or a come-on toward them. The family has been encouraging Lily to further her education, and she has been accepted into Harvard Business Law School in Boston. Rumors have it she wants to go to Duke University for the study of medicine and become a nurse.

Lily has a brother that is four years older than her, and his name is Thomas McCoy Stone V. Thomas is already at North Carolina State University, and he will major in horticulture in order to take on the family business and continue for many years in farming. The family wanted Lily to go to one of our country's finest college to study business law to help run the family's business to take over the finances and as a legal adviser. Time will tell how this saga of turn events will turn out with Lily wanting to go to medical school.

Thomas V and Lily both are experts at riding horses, and they have competed in many competitions and have won several trophies that now line their walls in the hallway of the house. Well, their Dad, Thomas IV, is so proud of his children; he had hallway lighting installed so the trophies were always highlighted as he wanted guest to enjoy the achievements of his kids. Their dad, Thomas IV, is also an expert rider and is credited with several trophies of his own.

Thomas III, grandpa to Thomas V and Lily, also enjoys being a part of the community and is a United States Senator for the ninth District of North Carolina. He is now a senior US Senator and has been for many years. He did run for governor for North Carolina twice and lost.

Many times in the late afternoon Lily would saddle up her horse named "Ben" and would take a one-hour ride through the country side if weather permitting. Often she would ride with Thomas V, but due to Thomas being in college she would ride alone, and sometimes with her dad if he was available.

Just like any other day which was a fall-of-the-year day with the temperature in the low 60s—almost perfect for riding. Lily was on her way. Along the trail she would stop periodically to rest Ben and enjoy the surrounding beauty of nature especially this time of the year with the changing of the leaves.

As she approaches the mossy creek area where she would always stop and water Ben, she saw a man from a distance who appeared to her to be fishing. It did not concern her much because she had encountered other fisherman along the trail many times. After watering Ben, she mounted Ben but noticed the man had left the area. She was a little concerned that she did not see in which direction he was headed.

Slowly, she and Ben were on their way going upstream and as always very thick underbrush for a little way then it opened into a clearing for about a mile. Just as she entered the underbrush, she heard a noise, and before she could react to the noise, this man grabbed her, pulled her off the horse. She was screaming, doing everything to kick the man, but he just overpowered her to point she could no longer fight back.

He bound her hands together, and the rope was tied to her neck as well. The man pulled her just about one quarter mile to an old pickup truck. He then put her in the floorboard so no one could see her and drove well over an hour and pulled into what she assumed was a farm and blindfolded her, so that she could not see her surroundings. He took her into a cellar where she could not be seen by anyone.

As nighttime was approaching, the family was getting somewhat concerned that Lily had not returned home. So several of the farmhands and her mother and dad all saddled up the horses; went out looking for her. They followed her trail that she took each day and found Ben near mossy creek but no sign of Lily. Nancy, Lily's mother rode back to the house and called the police and reported Lily was missing.

The police and several of the farmhands and her dad looked all night for her but to no avail. The next morning, the search continued one of the men found in the underbrush a shred of her clothing and on the ground with some evidence of a struggle. The police confirmed that someone had abducted her with the evidence that was found, and the trail led to where the truck was parked. They could see the footprints from both sides of the truck, and the tire tracks coming in and turning around and then leaving. With all the evidence found there was hardly any reason to continue with the search, but her dad and the farmhands continue to look for the next several days.

Thomas III came home from Washington to be a support for the family, but of course, there was nothing anyone could do but wait on some word from the police. After a three-week stay at home Thomas returned to Washington with the hopes that word would come in soon from the police about Lily's disappearance.

As Thomas started to go through his mail, he found a most unusual letter that was in Lily's hand writing stating that all is well with her, but he must have someone deliver $15,000 in cash to the post office in Asheville, North Carolina, on a designated day without the police and without contacting the police. If he and his family did not follow the instructions exactly, she would be killed instantly.

The family decided it was best to contact the police, and let them guide the family throughout the process. Much to everyone's surprise the news was leaked to the news media, and word got out to all parts of the country that a prominent North Carolinian senator's granddaughter was being held for ransom money.

The day came to deliver the money to the post office, and the money was placed in the exact spot that was requested—which was a container inside the post office. The family and police waited for hours as all eyes were on the container, no one showed up to claim the money.

The money was put into the container near the front entrance; it was on the left side of building. Their instructions were to wait for someone to claim the money. They would then hand over Lily after the person picking up the money was well out of sight. Many hours had passed, no one showed up so it was time to pick up the money and head back home thinking this was a hoax. As one of the undercover policeman when in to retrieve the money, lo and behold, the money was gone. How could this be? All eyes were on the container from the time it was put in until they went to retrieve the money.

The post office used the container for recycling waste paper until it was ready to be taken to the recycling center and they would push it through a trap door on the back side of the container into a large container outside. Several containers were stacked on top of each other so the containers were blocking any view of the trapdoor. None of the authorities knew about the trapdoor so it was easy for the person to pick up the money without being detected.

Days, weeks, and months past still no sign of Lily. Many of the folks in and around her community believed she was killed once the news media got word of her disappearance. Her family would never give up hope that she was still alive. Even the police were not hopeful that she was still alive.

Several months had passed since the abduction of Lily, so the family decided they would put out a notice to the newspapers throughout the country. The family was offering $5,000 reward money for an arrest to the person that had abducted her. As we all know when money is involved many people are vying to receive the money and especially that amount of money when times are hard.

Many tips were coming into the police department, so many in fact the police had to put out a statement: anyone found reporting false information would be arrested. This of course was to hold back so many false leads that were bogging down the police department chasing bad information.

One of the reports that came in was a woman's body that was found floating in the Catawba river near the Rozzelle's ferry landing that crossed over into Mecklenburg county. The body was an older lady that had walked away from a home that she was living in for retarded people.

Several sightings of young ladies about the same age of Lily came in that turned out to be just look-alikes. Some were in different parts of North Carolina, and some were in South Carolina. The most bizarre sighting was at a sideshow at a carnival in Atlantic City, New Jersey. The people that reported the person at the sideshow were the people that ran the show. They truly believed this was Lily because she joined the show a few months back, and they had seen in the newspaper Lily's disappearance and picture. This young lady looked about the same age and had that wonderful personality that was mention in the paper.

The people at the sideshow were very convincing to the police department in Lincoln county. This is truly Lily that is performing at their sideshow; that one of the policemen that knew Lily scheduled a trip to Atlantic City. The people at the side show were told not to say anything to anyone about the sighting so as not to scare off anyone that might be connected to the disappeared of Lily. They also said it would be in their best interest not to expose the information because if it is Lily and they would run then the side show people would lose out on the $5,000 reward money.

When officer Jack Lewis arrived in New Jersey, at the sideshow he saw the young lady. He was not sure because it had been almost one and half years the last time he saw her. The officer had to report the situation to the local authorities because officer Lewis did not have any jurisdiction in the state of New Jersey. Together they came up with a plan to watch this young lady when she was not on stage preforming.

The carnival was stationery to the Atlantic City area so the performing artists lived in and around the Atlantic City area. The police set up a plan to watch her living area with anyone coming in and out of the house. Two days went by but only the young lady was in and out. It was decided to confront the young lady, and her name was Sallie Fielding, twenty-two of age, a recent graduate of a performing art school in Newark, New Jersey. She wanted to start her career at the carnival in order to gain some experience before moving on to the theaters.

She was truly a look-alike of Lily and with the same bubbly personality. When officer Lewis showed Sallie the pictures of Lily, it was hard for her to believe how much they looked-alike.

CHAPTER 2

The White Oak Farm Is Being Established Late Seventeen Hundred

The first Thomas McCoy Stone was a United States senator for many years and was very well respected in the Halls of Congress and believed in horticulture so much that he was able to get some of the first bills passed in Congress for farmers. As you remember this predates the Civil War, and the government was still a fledgling, primitive government, and it was hard to achieve much in Washington during those days. Still the people were determined and had an insatiable desire to make a go of this country and the government as one body.

The farm was started on a small loan from a banker named J. D. Nixon in Charlotte who was a friend of Thomas. The two of them grew up together and lived on farms nearby where Thomas was starting his farm. Their families were sharecroppers and did not own the land, so none of the land was passed on to the next generation. Of course, Thomas had to put up the farm as collateral, but J. D. Nixon believed so strongly in the pursuit of Thomas's dream that it was easy to lend the money.

The farm was started with eighty-two acres of land. As the crop started coming in, and payments were being made to the bank to pay off the loan, Thomas was able to acquire more loans to purchase more land. After about ten years the farm grew to 4,300 acres making it one of the largest farms in North Carolina if not one of the largest in the southeast.

Not much was known about the slaves on the farm, but what we do know is they were hard-working, and they gave a lot to the growth of the farm and the production of the crops. No records were kept concerning the slaves, but there were some sketchy notes made about them, and it was believed that somewhere between fifteen and twenty slaves worked the farm. As the farm grew, so did the population of the slaves grew to work the farm, but there again it is not known exactly how many slaves were working the farm once it reached its potential of 4,300 acres.

It is believed that the slaves on the white oak farm were treated much better than most slave owners treated their workers, and therefore, word had spread among the slave population that it would be better to work for the White Oak Farm than any others in the area. Some of the slave owners' theory was to split up the families in order to get better production out of them, but as the Stone family found out by leaving the family together created loving and happy families, for better productivity of the slave, so therefore, they were treated differently than other slave owners treated their workers.

Slave Houses on the White Oak Farm

It was believed by the Stone family that no one should ever be enslaved by another person, but by Thomas realizing the situation for the slaves, it was almost impossible for them not to be part of white families. How would they support their own families without jobs, no housing, and they did not own any land to be farmers?

For the most part, the slave families at White Oak Farm had good housing and were given good food to eat, enough to sustain them for their hard work on the farm. Most importantly, the slaves were given their freedom to worship and hold a congregation Sunday-worship service. Most were devout Christians and believed in the gospel and worshiped and praised God through their singing, not only on Sunday but during the day as they worked to manage the corps and the farm.

Thomas Stone was a good businessman. He worked hard to preserve his good name and reputation throughout the community.

Most of all he lived by the word of God and believed deeply in the golden rule of God (to do unto others as you would have others do unto you). Thomas had three children; two of which were boys and one daughter. Thomas, being a good father, did instill in his three children the golden rule and how to be nice and kind to others.

During a civic meeting among some of the leaders of the local counties held in the small town in Lincolnton, North Carolina, Thomas II was able to meet his future wife Trudy. It was a meeting where Thomas's dad and Trudy's dad both knew one another very well from past political gatherings and each had an admiration for each other.

It was a warm sunny day of early spring with the temperature about 75 degrees and warm enough to make everyone feel a little sleepy after a most satisfying lunch. The meeting, lunch, and entertainment were all held on the grounds at a church near downtown Lincolnton, and it was known for holding political rallies for both parties. But of course, this meeting brought both parties together and was all about learning from each other to help better their own community.

Thomas describes the first encounter with Trudy as a not so friendly meeting because the two of them were paired up with each other for a sack race. The elder women were in-charge of the entertainment consisting of the younger adults. So as it turned out, Thomas and Trudy were paired together; Trudy was highly competitive and was determined to win the sack race come hell or high water.

When the two were positioned in the sack together at the starting line, Trudy could not stand still and was constantly pulling on the bag; she was ready to go and could not wait for the person to say "go." As they started off, only a few feet away from the starting line, Thomas fell because of Trudy pulling on the sack. By the time the two of them were standing up again the race was over for the other contestants. Of course, Thomas was ready to come out of the sack and call it quits. Trudy said, "Oh no, you don't. We started this race together we are going to finish it together." Once they had the sack in place again, off they go until they crossed the finish line.

Everyone was cheering them for finishing the race even though dead last in the race. Trudy was so mad and disappointed they came in last that she was shouting at Thomas for not being more of a man to do better. She was in his face, pointing her finger at him saying things like. "You have no competitive spirit, and you don't care about anybody but yourself."

Well, Thomas had enough of the screaming that he grabbed Trudy and put a kissing on her like she never had. Trudy stepped back and looked at Thomas as if to say, you're not going to outdo me, grabbed him and put a kissing on him like he never had. While all of this was going on, almost everyone was watching as the two of them slowly separated their arms from around each other knowing this was the start of something—a wonderful "love affair." Thomas said to Trudy, "I like your competitive nature and that you will make someone a good wife." Of course, Trudy had to have the last word and said to Thomas, "What do you mean a good wife? I will be a wonderful wife because I have the desire?"

The two of them spent the rest of the afternoon together. Thomas was on his way to Gastonia to see Trudy as many times as he could. They were sending letters back and forth almost on a daily bases. Both were big into keeping all of the love letters. Many years later, the letters became part of rich history of the Stone family which was displayed at the White Oak farmhouse, so that everyone could enjoy them.

Almost two years later, as Trudy was completing her education, the two were married in the Trudy family's Methodist Church in Gastonia and spent their two-day honeymoon in Charlotte and then returned to the White Oak Farm.

Thomas McCoy II wanted to carry on the business of the farm while his brother Woodrow Cameron was more interested in becoming a banker in New York City and did pursue his dream and then moved on to Kansas City, Missouri, where he became president and CEO of the Missouri-Kansas Bank. Everyone called him Woody, and the childhood name stayed with him throughout his life. On the other hand, Sarah Ellen was more in love with the thought and attracted in becoming a mother and lives for her children throughout her life. Sarah Ellen did well for herself and married into a wonderful and most wealthy family, and as it turned out, her husband was a two-time governor for the state of Virginia.

Thomas Senior had it documented through the court system. The children who took on the ownership of the farm would inherit most of the stock of the farm in order to continue with the farm for many years to come. This also included the offspring of the next generations. Thomas Senior was born in 1779 and lived until 1859 being eighty when he passes away at which time Thomas II took over the family farm.

The farm did well and continued to grow under the leadership of Thomas II and his wife Andrea Truesdale Stone. As Andrea was growing up it just seem fitting to call her Trudy for short. So after she was married and living at the farm, the slaves began to call her Miss Trudy. Thomas II and Trudy had one young daughter and her name was Candice Diana Stone named after her grandmother Stone. Grandmother Candice Stone was so delighted when her name was being passed on to her granddaughter. Candice has two slightly older brothers, of course, the oldest being Thomas McCoy Stone III, and the younger LeRoy Rogers Stone. LeRoy was named after his mother's father, Mr. LeRoy Lee Rogers. LeRoy was a two-term mayor in the town of Gastonia and also a state legislature.

3
CHAPTER

Atmosphere of Civil War Looming

Some dark days lie ahead for the farm as the atmosphere of a civil war was rapidly looming. Thomas II and his father had discussed the possibility of a civil war before his death, and the two of them did some planning in the event that it did come about. They knew the Union troops would be hard to hold back, and if they would run the farm with their soldiers they would take all the food and leave very little for the family and for the slave families.

At a nearby cave on the bank of mossy rock stream that was fed by runoff water coming down from the mountains was an ideal location. It gave an ideal location for hiding food and other valuables for the family. The cave was so well hidden especially in the summertime when all the foliage was on the trees. A person would need to be looking for it to be able to see it.

Planning went into keeping the slave families safe as well, and the cave was large enough to fit all the slaves into it along with the food and other items that the family wanted to make sure they held onto. No one knew how and what would take place if and when the Northern Union troops came or what to expect from the Confederate troops as well. It was thought it was better to be safe than sorry if one did not plan well.

The slaves were not comfortable about going into the cave because it was thought that prehistoric man used the cave for shelter many hundred years ago because bones from humans were found on the inside of it along with primitive tools and weapons. The slaves were finally convinced they would be better off to go into the cave rather than face any bad things that may happen to them with the Union troops or the Confederate troops.

Preparation was in place to board up the entrance to the cave making it tight enough where animals and rats and bats and other wild animals could not get into the food and destroy it. Once the boarding was in place they would start to move in some of the items such as bedding along with some food. Lookout points were in place in four locations of the farm to warn of any movements from Union troops or Confederate troops. These lookout points would be manned twenty-four hours a day and far enough away from the house where it would give the people time to use the designated escape route for getting to the cave area.

An ingenious signaling device was used to notify the people around the house that impending troops were marching in by using rope-twine tied to cow bells in trees near the house and linked to each lookout area. Four different trees were used with cow bells, so that the families would know in which direction the troops were coming in. The lookout person would ring the bell three times for Union troops and four times for the Confederates.

Plans were in place in the event the slaves were freed and how to handle the people once they were freed. The slaves would be given housing; they are currently using on the grounds of the farm until they could establish living quarters elsewhere. Thomas II decided it would be best if the White Oak Farm would donate a certain amount of acreage to each of the slave families in order to get started farming and supporting themselves. This acreage would be located on the northwest side of the forty-three hundred acres, and it would be somewhere between ten and fifteen acres per family. Each family would be responsible for building their own living quarters once the acreage was established for them.

Of course, losing each of the slaves meant a devastating blow to the White Oak Farm. All the eligible people old enough to work would be offered a job with pay on the farm, so that it could continue as a business. This means the farm would need to borrow money from the bank in order to pay the workers. It was thought that times would be especially hard after the war, and it may not be so easy to borrow money.

All of this were plans, and no one would know the outcome, but at least they had a plan in place.

Word spread rapidly as the first shots were fired April 12, 1861, at Fort Sumter, and the Union Army was forced to surrender, and the Fort was taken over by the Confederacy Army. It only took two days for word to reach the White Oak Farm that the first shots were fired for the start of the Civil War. This news only hastens the resolve of the White Oak Farm to gear up strongly in self-defense of their preservation for the farm.

Many months passed and news was coming in from time to time about the war, but life on the farm was pretty normal except several of the younger male slaves were heading off to join the Union Army to fight against slavery. No one saw this coming until one night under the cover of darkness three young guys took off, but five were in the schedule to go, but two decided at the last minute not to go.

As the months rolled by, tension got even tighter with the slaves, and some just wanted to leave the farm and start their own journey of life. But many were frightened of running into the Confederate Army and hanged on the spot as runaway slaves. So most of the slaves stayed put until after the war.

A little more than a year had passed after the start of the war, when late in the evening of June 15 after a heavy downpour of rain which left the area very humid and hot. At a distant from the north-west lookout station coming down the old wagon trail which is now highway 103, were sounds like a very low thunder were men on horseback; some horse-drawn wagons as well as some cannons and what looked like a thousand men walking. The lookout person had to wait a little longer to get a close-up view of the troops.

Sure enough it was the Union Army coming, and cold chills were running down the spine of the lookout person and nervous so much so it was hard for him to run over were the rope twine that was located to warn the others. He was saying to himself, do I have this right it is the Union Army with blue uniforms? What he could see was the men with rifles which looked to be ten feet long, and as they were marching the men were singing hymns, and suddenly the army just stopped. Everyone just sat down as if they were taking a break from the late afternoon humidity and hot weather.

The lookout person did ring the cow bell and the slaves started their undercover marching in the designated area toward the cave in order to stay away from the eyes of the Union troops. Some of the slaves were left inside and outside the house so it would not look so suspicious that other slaves were part of the farm.

The Union Troops, recognizing the farm was close by and after their break, marched into the farm area of the house. The troops were ordered to set up their tents for the evening. Several officers and several solders came to the house. The commanding officer was Henry Ferguson III.

Thomas II was told to gather all of his family and farm hands and bring each of them to the front of the house. Each of them was stood in a single line and as the commanding officer started to speak. He walked back and forth in front of them always with his right hand resting on his sword as to show who was in charge.

He explained that none of his men were to be mistreated or shown any disrespect, it would be act of aggression against his men, and therefore, each of them would be classified as enemies against the Union Army. Any person or persons found guilty of an act of aggression would be shot. He went on to say that the farm would be a resting area for his troops.

The house and farm would be left unharmed when they departed for their journey southward. The house would be headquarters for the officers and sleeping quarters for the commanding officers. Thomas II was told they would need to make other arrangements for his family's sleeping areas. He was told also the troops would take most of the food for the troops, and no harm would come to them as long as the family and farm hands corporates. All the women including Miss Trudy were told to prepare an evening meal for his officers. He also said that he expected breakfast at six the next morning.

As the troops were setting up and preparing their tents, some of the men responsible for the cannons placed them in a redoubt-semi-circle position, like a fortified fortress in the event of an attack. All of the saddles were removed from the horses and led out to the pasture for grazing.

Some of the officers were getting suspicious about the amount of housing for slaves surrounding the farm house without slaves to fill them. Many questions were being asked as to how it was possible to work such a large farm without more slaves. Each time Thomas was trying to defuse the questions without telling lies; he would say that at the start of the Civil War some farm hands decided to go and join the Union Army in order to fight for their freedom.

After about four days of the siege on the farm a scuffle broke out between one of the slaves and one of the soldiers. The slave had accidentally trip over the soldier equipment and fell across the soldier causing the soldier to become angry. Thomas II was nearby and was able to stop a fight knowing the slave would be shot. Nothing was ever said about it and life returned to normal.

After the six day the family was waking up too much noise: hearing the men moving around, horses were being gathered equipment was being picked up, and tents were being folded. Could this be the day the family was looking for when all the men were moving on? As the family stepped outside to see all the commotion, they could see that much of their food was being loaded onto the wagons.

So the thoughts were running through Thomas II's mind was thank goodness the planning paid off, and that by storing some of the food in the cave was going to save them from starvation even if they had to ration out the food until they could regain their normal stockpile of food. It took the troops almost three hours to start their journey southward. Once the troops were way past their eyesight then it was time to notify the slaves that were in the cave it was safe to come out.

The slaves were thankful for the planning to keep everyone safe, but it's no time to let down their guard. The war was still going on and intensifying: anything could happen. So all the lookout areas were once again manned and the same procedure would be followed. Life on the farm started returning to day-to-day routine of working the farm, and some of the food were starting to be replenished. The slaves were starting to return to their Sunday worship service and praising the Lord for their safe passage during the siege from the Union troops.

Things were going so well there were talks at the farm about doing away with the four lookout positions around the farm, but Miss Trudy was still uneasy about the war as it was still going on and insisted the lookouts be left in position with guards. Well, Miss Trudy was right after all, on the early morning of March 1, 1865 a small band of Confederate garrisons were spotted coming up the old dirt road which is highway 103.

The southeast lookout person heard the commotion as they approached the farm. Could it be the Confederate this time it sure look different than the Union Army? Sure enough it was the Confederate Army, so the lookout person ran fast so he could ring the bell four times: this time the Confederate Army. Once again the slaves took their position inside the cave as the approaching army descended upon the farm. But this time things were a little different as the commanding officer was under strict orders to meet up with General Robert E. Lee's Army in Appomattox, Virginia.

The garrison consisted of 160 men and again they took as much food as their wagons could haul. Once the food was loaded which took about four hours and the horses were watered down they were on their way. After about two hours had passed to make sure none of the units would return for any reason, the slaves in the cave were notified it was time to return to the farm.

Civil War Statistics and Slavery Abolished: What to Do with Freedom

Large populated cities and towns on both sides of the Mason Dixon by 1861 were targets. The Union and Confederate commanders made the capture or destruction of enemy cities a central feature of their campaigns, why?

- By advancing into and occupying enemy territory, armies destroyed the geographic integrity of their adversaries, a major step in destroying their will to fight.
- Most Americans assumed that the fall of capital cities—Washington, District of Columbia; and Richmond, Virginia—would mean victory for one side and defeat for the other.
- Because these cities had manufacturing and storage centers within their borders. Bombarding and setting fire to cities also destroyed factories, foundries, supply depots, and warehouses. Interrupt or incapacitate the enemy's ability to arm, feed, and clothe themselves and the war ends.
- Burning cities damaged civilian morale, "bringing the enemy to the point where it can go no further physically or emotionally."

Some of the cities that were hardest hit and destroyed were: Atlanta Charleston, South Carolina; Columbia, South Carolina.; and Richmond, Virginia. For the most part these cities would need to be rebuilt before normal life could once again advance forward. It would take years before the healing process would begin, and all the people that were affected by the war could start to; (forget, and forgive).

As most Americans came to the understanding what the war was all about was twofold:

- To keep our nation together as one union and government as Abraham Lincoln had so gallantly stated during his speeches.
- Abolish slavery so that every man, woman, and child could walk in this country as a free person.

Roughly the number of American soldiers that died in the Civil War was 620,000. This amounted to 2 percent of the population at the time of the Civil War. Hundreds died of disease.

The Confederacy included the states of Texas, Arkansas, Louisiana, Tennessee, Mississippi, Alabama, Georgia, Florida, South Carolina, North Carolina, and Virginia. Jefferson Davis was their President.

Maryland, Delaware, West Virginia, Kentucky and Missouri were called Border States.

The Union included the states of Maine, New York, New Hampshire, Vermont, Massachusetts, Connecticut, Rhode Island, Pennsylvania, New Jersey, Ohio, Indiana, Illinois, Kansas, Michigan, Wisconsin, Minnesota, Iowa, California, Nevada, and Oregon.

Enlistment strength for the Union Army is 2,672,341 which can be broken down as:

1. 2,489,836 white soldiers
2. 178,975 African American soldiers
3. 3,530 Native American troops

Enlistment strength for the Confederate Army ranges from 750,000 to 1,227,890.

Several days passed after the peace agreement between the north and south was signed on April 9, 1865 at Appomattox, Virginia, the war was over when news reaches the White Oak Farm. Happy days would be had by all on the farm especially the back people.

All slaves were given their freedom, but on the White Oak Farm mixed emotions for black people because of how they were treated so very well compared to the other Negro slaves on other farms. Life must go on and new things must be put in place. Thomas II asked that his family members and the free slaves assemble the next morning after breakfast in front of the farmhouse. After a night of sleeping on his thoughts concerning the war and what it stood for:

He began by saying, "We all have heard a lot about the war and many prayers have been said, and we have only experienced a little at the farm during the war but we all have endured. It is now time to put our arms around another new part of life and embrace the change with gratitude and love for each other. Times will be hard for next while for the farm and for the people of color but it the duty of the farm to put a plan in place that will help all us as we move forward."

Thomas II told of the discussion with his father before he passed away, and how his dad was passionate about making sure the slaves families were as secure as possible if war took place and if the slaves were freed.

They we're welcome to stay on and use the housing on the farm until they could find a more suitable place to live. They would be paid for their labor on the farm. Any families with a desire to start their own farm would be offered ten and up fifteen areas of land which would be located on the northwest side of the White Oak Farm. For the farm, it would mean the farm would need to borrow the money in order to pay the farmhands if money would be available through the banks.

Many months has passed since the Civil War ended, and many of the slave families have moved onto other areas, and three families took up the offer of land acreage donated by the Stone family. Many of the blacks that moved were nearby and continued to work at the farm. Thomas II was able to secure a loan because of the farm's reputation from the same bank in Charlotte that his father used many years ago when he was buying land. When the crops were coming in, the farm was able to start paying the loan down and the farmhands were being paid for their work for the first time.

By the time the war was over, Thomas II's children were starting to get a little older, and their help was needed on the farm. Thomas III was now seventeen and training had already started when he was fourteen in learning how to do many of the things that keeps the farm running. Thomas III was a good-looking, tall, young man with very dark hair and is a highly intelligent person.

During social events, many of the young ladies would just smother him with attention, always trying to lure him in their direction. It was thought perhaps that Thomas III would marry early in life because of all the attention from so many women. He was always overwhelmed with the attention, but he knew he should stay focus on the farm duties and not get too involved with young ladies. Back in the early days living on a farm, it was not easy to get an education from public school, so it was his mother that did the home schooling for all three children. It was now time to start thinking about college and where he wants to go to school.

Thomas III had an older cousin named Lauren Rice which he corresponded with for several years. She was just finishing up at a college in Washington, DC, named Columbian College and the name was changed to Columbian University in 1873 and many years later changed to George Washington University in 1904. Thomas III was so inspired to further his education applied at Columbian University and was accepted.

He told his parent that the White Oak Farm blood runs through his veins the same as it does for his dad and grandfather, but he must quench a thirsty desire to be a missionary either in India or Africa. Also he was looking forward to seeing Washington, DC and some of the things his grandfather told him about before his death. Because his grandfather was a congressman he had many good things to say about the great city.

Thomas told of the corresponding letters with his cousin Lauren Rice that she sent to him about the school in Washington. A Baptist missionary and leading minister, Luther Rice raised funds to purchase a site in Washington, DC, and the school was commissioned by President Monroe to start the small college in 1821. Of course, Luther Rice was Lauren Rice's grandfather, and she wanted to carry on the tradition by attending where her grandfather helped start many years ago. This, of course, fueled the fire in Thomas III's soul because it was the missionary training for his mission trips that he so desired. Lauren's grandfather, Luther, was a missionary in India back before the college was started.

Now LeRoy Rogers was just fifteen, and it was time for him to start learning the ends, ins, and outs of the farm. but his dad had already detected some trouble areas with LeRoy that he just could not connect with the day-to-day routine of farm duties. LeRoy was eager to learn but not the farm. His mind was always into books and any time the family could not find LeRoy he was always some place reading.

His grandfather had collected some of the earliest history books on the Revolutionary War and the American history. The more LeRoy read about the military the more he wanted to learn. He had remembered both the Union army and Confederate army coming to their house, and how he was inspired by their guns, ammunition, uniforms, horses, and cannon. Even at a young age, he just knew this was for him for all the soldiers were very orderly and very direct in their mannerism.

Their mother, Miss Trudy, was trained early on as a teacher and how important it was to start the reading and learning at a very young age and making the young minds hungry for knowledge. She spent countless hours reading to them and teaching them how to read. As one can say the proof is in pudding when it comes to LeRoy as he was the one that could read and retain things better than his siblings.

Well, Thomas II sure needed LeRoy's help around on the farm but did not want to discourage him from reading. A time was set aside to talk with LeRoy. Between Miss Trudy and himself they were able to implement a schedule for LeRoy so as not to take all of his reading time up with chores, but he was expected to complete the chores first.

As expected, LeRoy took it like a man when his parents told him what his first duties were of the day. In his young mind he took on the new rules as a challenge and thought that he could get his chores done early and spend the rest of his time reading like he wanted to do. He stood up straight and tall; said to them he would do as he was told to do. He also told his parent his desire was to read every book in his grandfather's library.

Now that was going to be a real challenge because his grandfather spent more than sixty years collecting his books. His book collection was one of the largest private collections in the country.

On the other hand, Candice Diana was just turning thirteen and was wide open and just eager to learn and help any way she could. Her mother, Miss Trudy, was very proud of her and encourages Candice: knowing that with her attitude she probably would want to stay on the farm and help manage it in years to come, but it was still too early to predict Candice's future, but she was determined to please her parents.

As the years progressed after the Civil War, life was returning to normal and many of the areas of the country were rebuilding because of the destruction from the war. Still there were raw feelings between the black and white people, and as time marched on, the black people were still suppressed by the whites. The Stone family did everything they could to keep down turmoil between the blacks and the whites, but still the hard feeling were there among the blacks.

Thomas III would soon be leaving for Washington, DC, and there was some rail service between Atlanta and Washington, DC, with stops along the way in Columbia, South Carolina, Charlotte, North Carolina, and Richmond, Virginia. His family had to take him to Charlotte to the train station there for his journey to the north. Of course, Miss Trudy, being a good mother, had enough food to last him what looked like a week's supply. But that is what mothers are all about and thank goodness for them.

Being eighteen was exciting, Thomas III had never been on a train before was so excited, just like being a kid all over again that he could not sleep the night before. He was looking forward to the school, and seeing DC. The newly constructed Union Train Station in Washington was located near the ongoing construction of the United States Capitol Building. His cousin Lauren had written to him about the new Union Station and about the construction of US Capitol Building. Also with the work going on about the much talked-about Washington Monument that was started before the war and being resumed now as they find the stone, some from each state.

After a few weeks past for Thomas at school, a young lady by the name of Francesca De Mayo Esposito, an Italian decent, caught his eye. Now back at home the ladies swapped Thomas III with attention, but this lady really caught his eye: she was so different from all that he knew in the past. Every time he would look her way it was like he did not exist. He said to himself, "What is it with this lady? In the past, ladies smothered me with attention, and she will not even look at me?"

As the weeks passed, so did Thomas III's curiosity for Francesca attention multiple into almost a secret love affair. This was all new to Thomas III, and the feeling he had in the bottom of his stomach for this most gorgeous woman. He had never seen anyone like her before; one so beautiful with long black hair, dark-complexed skin, tall, and her moves were like the rhythm of music. "I have got to find a way to get her attention without it being so obvious."

The day had come to either make a fool of himself or be struck with overwhelming fascination with each other. He approached her as they were walking to class and decided this was the moment of truth. Thomas III said to her, "Fran," as everyone called her. "My name is Thomas McCoy Stone III, and I am from the state of North Carolina, and may I walk alongside you as we make our way to class?"

She agreed as she told her name and that she was from the state of New Jersey and that her grandparents had emigrated from Italy.

He said to her, "I am not a shy person, but I must tell you every time I wanted to talk to you it's like I had all these butterflies in my stomach because you never looked my way."

She explained that at a very young age, she was taught the importance to always stay within her ethnic group of friends and especially young men. She went on to say that she knew of his interest in her because she would see him from the corner of her eye watching her.

Thomas said to her, "I would be most horned if you would accompany me in a Saturday afternoon walk through the city and see some the construction, statues, and landmarks."

She would ask permission from her house-mother at the university, and they would meet up at the main entrance at 12:30 p.m. or shortly after lunch. They both were glad about their conversation with each other, but it was time for class. During their walk, she told of her interest in Thomas, but she was still obligated to respect her parents' wishes to stay within the ethnic group of Italians. As time passed, so did the two of them remain good friends and spent much time with each other.

Now the day had come for Thomas to depart for his missionary trip to Peru, South America. Mixed emotions on the part of Fran and Thomas as the time was drawing near. Thomas was doing his best to understand her obligation to her family, but once again, the moment of truth was upon him, and he must tell her his true feelings. He held her close and with a gentle kiss told Fran, "From this day forward I will always love you, and it started from the first time I sat eye on you." Fran did not reciprocate with "I love you too," but her loving smile and closeness was enough for Thomas to know she would be waiting for him to return in about a year from his mission trip.

LeRoy was now eighteen years old, and he was looking at his future of joining the military as a young cadet at West Point Academy and has already been appointed by the US Congressman from North Carolina. Once again his parents were on their way to the train station in Charlotte to send off their second child headed north. The train will carry him as far as New York City. Beyond the big city, he must ride in a horse-drawn carriage to West Point which is sixty miles or a nine-hour ride with changes in the two horse teams about every fifteen miles. LeRoy will stay overnight in the city, and start his long journey north by horse and carriage at daybreak. Five other new cadets would also make the journey to West Point on the same carriage with LeRoy.

The carriage driver, named Sam Perkins, turned out to be a graduate of the West Point many years ago and served in the military during the Civil War as a Union soldier. As he retired from the military, he wanted so much to stay on at the academy that he was willing take on the job driving the cadets back and forth to New York City as needed. The pay was not very good, but he was able to still be a part of the ever day routines. The academy and military was all the family that Sam had left. LeRoy was absolutely overwhelmed by excitement with all that Mr. Perkins was telling them about the academy that he could hardly wait to arrive and get down to the business of being a cadet.

As they arrived at the academy, what LeRoy and the other saw was a line of cadets in full uniform standing at ease as if they waiting on the new cadets to arrive. Mr. Perkins pulled in front what looked like a thousand cadets. Mr. Perkins did not tell them about the business of the upperclassmen coming out to greet them as they stepping off the carriage.

As each new cadet was fully standing on the ground all the upper classmen came up to greet them in way that they had never been greeted before, and they will never forget. They were screaming and telling the new cadets they were lowlife and all were trash underneath their feet and why were they there trying to dirty up and stink up their workplace and home? LeRoy and the others were thinking this is not a good way to greet a new set of cadets that is willing be a part of this great academy.

When all the screaming was over the new cadets were told to not ask questions and follow the three men that was standing to left side of the formation; they would lead them to their new home. As they entered into their new living quarter they were told again they are low-life and did not have a brain of their own and they would be told everything to do from this day forward.

The three men told the new cadets they were their guardian angels, and each we're expected to do as they were told to do. Any of the men caught crying will be stood in front of the whole cadet body of men and then they will be called mommy's boy. Being a part of the academy means they are men and not boys any longer and will be treaty as men.

LeRoy, thought, *I come here to learn how to be a good cadets and the only thing they want to do is scream and tell us how bad we all are.* His mother and father were always good to him, and his sibling and he were not used to the screaming as it seems to go on forever. But over time he and the others began to realize the behavior was all part of their training as they grew into their position as cadets. No doubt about it, they felt like lowlife, but one thing for sure they knew who was boss.

One year later, Thomas III was returning from his mission trip from Peru, South America, back to the college in Washington where he could not wait to see Francesca. He knew that she would be waiting on the same platform at Union station where he left her standing as the train pulled away from the station on his mission trip.

As the train was nearing the station, Thomas was able to put his head out the window, so that she could see him, and he could see her. His heart was beating fast, and he could hardly breathe with so much excitement. He had never been as nervous as he was at this moment in time. When the train was pulling into the station area. he could not see Fran. Was she late or was she not able come to greet him? Now his heart dropped to his stomach as if someone had died. Could it be that she had found another while he was away, he did not think so, something else must be wrong he just felt it in his heart?

As Thomas made his way to the college and his sleeping quarters, he found a letter lying on his bunk addressed to him. As he opened the letter, he knew something was badly wrong, and as the tears started to swell in eyes, the letter started by saying:

"My Dearest and most Precious Friend Thomas…"

It went on to say that she was called home by her mother two months before Thomas scheduled return due to a severe illness of her dad. Their family had a thriving bakery in Jersey City, New Jersey, and that her mother needed help running the bakery while her mother cared for her dad. She had much to say in the letter, but her closing words were,

My life has been enhanced more than one
could ever find words to express with your kind-

ness and gentle breath touches of love that comes from the bottom of your heart."

I will forever remain your friend until my last breath of life in me.

Francesca

Thomas sent several letters to Fran from the address that she supplied in the letter to Thomas, but he never heard back from her. So over time he knew she was too involved with the family and family business, and of course, he was most disappointed, but being a part of a family business himself he understood.

His studies must go on and the same for a new love adventure with hopes one day to find someone of equal qualities as Fran, but he knew too those were big shoes to fill. Time passed, and time has come to graduate and move back to the farm which he was looking forward to seeing his family and getting back to working the farm.

By now Candice Diana was now turning eighteen and was ready to start her own adventures of life, but it seem that she had already found the love of her life but was not ready to marry. She was taking a more active role in the farm and wanted to learn from her dad the finance end of the business, so that she could help her brother Thomas in running the farm when it comes time. Candice was always wide open with her activities, and as her dad would always say, "she does not let any grass grow underneath her feet."

Thomas III arrived back home a couple weeks after graduation and found the farm had changes: it looked cleaner and brighter than he left it four years ago. There seems to be more workers; an array of cattle so many he could not count them all. His dad decided to get into the dairy business because there was more demand for milk not only for drinking and butter, as well as for food processing throughout the region.

The farm had plenty of grazing pastures for the cows, so why not put the land to good use and help the farm financially. Of course, having so many milk cows it required many more workers to put the cows into the barn and spread straw, so the cows would eat and stand still during the milking which was twice a day.

Thomas made his way to his old room of the house and started to put away his belongings and suddenly looked out the window which was facing the front side of the house. As he was looking out, he could just vision for a few moments Francesca walking across the yard with her beautiful long black hair gently blowing in the afternoon spring breeze. When love comes knocking at your door and it goes away, it is hard to forget the special moments in time. A reflection of time, of course, but it was time to move on in life and settle down to farm life once again.

For Thomas III, life was characterized by starting over again at the farm and now learning some of the new routines of the farm procedures and learning how to be a dairyman as well. When he left for Washington four years ago, the farm only had three old milk cows, and they were used for the family and workhands.

Some of workers' duties were to show Thomas III how to round up the cows for milking early in the morning around 6:00 a.m. and again around 6:00 p.m. This timing for milking gave the cow's milksacks time to maximize the holding of milk and to relieve the burden on the cows of holding the milk. Not only did he learn the process of milking, he also had to learn the process of making butter which was a big part of the farm business.

One day as he was relaxing from all the work he decided well once again he would send off another letter to Francesca knowing it would take about two weeks for the letter to reach her. This time in thirty days a letter came, and Thomas was overwhelmed with excitement.

My dear friend, Thomas,

Many things had happened when I last saw you and held you in my arms. My dad passed away, and of course, my mother needs me even more with the bakery, so that we are able to support our large family of eight siblings of which I am next to the oldest. As my dad was taking his last breath of life, he made me promised that

I would not marry outside the Italian bloodline of people, which of course, I did make that last promise to him.

I have yet to marry, but there is a young man that I am interested in, but no one could ever equal your quality of kindness, gentleness, and compassion.

Forever your friend,

Francesca

For LeRoy he was now in his third year at West Point and now classified as an upperclassman and will be able to give the wonderful greeting as new cadets arrive for duty. He has already established his duties as a full-time soldier once he has been commission as an officer of the United States Army. He has notified his parents, brother, and sister that he has no desire to return to the farm to take up any responsibilities of caring for the farm in any fashion. He has asked for their understanding as he will be a full-time soldier as a commission officer in the United States Army. He wished them well in their endeavor as they carry out and continue with the family farm.

Thomas III was starting to socialize once again with the homegrown ladies of the region and many had already married. but a few were still single, and of course all, were vying for his attention once again. His thoughts were to try and find the right person because his first love was so easy with her personality, sweetness, kindness, and her radiant beauty. Could it be possible to find such a person with such outstanding charters as was Francesca? Only time will tell as he singles out by getting to know the ladies one by one.

On a hot summer day as he was making his way into Denver, North Carolina, on the wagon for some supplies, he stopped at a nearby farm to water the horses. He saw standing near the barn a lady with long dark hair, and from the distant he thought for a moment it was Francesca. As he was watering the horses, she turned and caught a glimpse of him looking at her. Thomas looked and looked again. Could this be the one?

He tied the reins of the horses to the watering trough and walked over to greet her, and as he approached her, he noticed a wedding ban on the ring finger. Being a good neighbor he introduced himself to her; told her his intention of being there. She introduced herself as Rachel Benfield Seifert. Her and her husband had bought the farm about two years ago for a modest amount of money from her uncle Tom Benfield.

"We were looking forward to many happy years working the farm and raising horses." she said.

Thomas said he remembered Tom Benfield and did not know he moved away because he had been in college and on a mission trip for the last four years. She went on to say that her husband had fallen ill to some unknown disease that the doctors could not cure. Thomas offered his support with anything he could do to help her and her family as he was departing and thanked her for the water for himself and for the horses.

Two months went by and during a Sunday worship service, Thomas looked to his left and spotted Rachel sitting alone and wondered why she was by herself. He thought perhaps the couple had children. As the service concluded, Thomas walked over to Rachel to be neighborly once again and said to her, "I hope all is well with you and your family."

She started by saying her husband had passed away almost two months ago and his body, at his request, was sent back to the Amish area in Ohio outside of Canton where he was raised. He was not Amish but loves the Amish people during his childhood. She herself was from the Northwest Conner of West Virginia not far from the Ohio area. She told Thomas they did not have any children and that not having children make it easy on her and the rest of the family to cope with his death.

After talking with her for a while, he felt a breath of fresh air sweep over him as if he had known her for a long time, and she was not like the other loquacious ladies of the area: all down to earth with her mannerisms and kindness. Of course, he did not want to appear hasty because of the death of her husband, but he knew he wanted to get to know her better.

As he started to walk away, Thomas turned toward her once again and said, "Would you like to visit the White Oak Farm one day? I know you love horses because of your farm, and you can give me and my dad some tips on how to get started with riding horses on our farm." Thomas went on to say the only horses they have on the farm are workhorses, but he and his dad wanted to get more involved with saddle horses and breeding.

The two of them set up a day in which she could visit the farm; it would be on Saturday of the same week due to his dad's business trip to Raleigh, and he was due back home on Friday. Thomas said that he would ride over and pick her up in the small carriage, but she said she would ride over on her favorite horse named "Mo" to give the horse some good exercise.

Thomas was excited to have a chance to spend some time with Rachel, and as she arrived, his parents were there to greet her along with Candice. She was invited to have an early lunch with the family, but as it turned out, the lunch went into almost three hours as they got to know one another. Rachel was excited about sharing her knowledge of riding horses with the family and offered her help as the farm started to move in the direction of buying and caring for the horses.

Rachel asks Thomas to show her around the farm, so that she could get acquainted with the layout and where a good area would be for the horses as they arrived. The two of them must have walked two hours or more around the farm. Thomas could feel there was a friendship that had started to develop, but he knew not to push too hard toward anything more. He kept saying to himself that time will heal the loss of her husband, and he will never cross the line of the heeling process.

Many months had passed, Thomas and Rachel were spending some time together, and the farm was getting ready for a couple of saddle horses as Rachel was there to assist as they arrived. Thomas was not much on riding except for riding bareback on the old workhorses back when he was a kid, and his dad would throw him and LeRoy up and they would head down the dirt road.

It would not take long before Rachel would have Thomas in the saddle and sure enough she showed up one day and asked if he had time to ride for a while. The two them toured the White Oak Farm on horseback and into some areas that Thomas had never seen before. They were following the mossy creek bed, and Thomas wanted to show Rachel the cave where the slaves were sheltered during the Civil War to keep them safe during raids on the farm.

As they approached the cave. Thomas and Rachel dismantled the horses for watering.

Rachel said to Thomas, "You have heard my stories of life, and I have helped guide you and your family with the riding horses, but Thomas I know very little about you. I see the ladies at church swamp you with attention, and you have so many opportunities with the ladies, but you don't seem to be interest any of them. Why not?"

Thomas told her the story of Francesca, and how he fell in love, but it was not to be. He went on to say, "The ladies around in this area are a "dime a dozen," but none of them measure up to your standard of kindness, sweetness, compassion, not to mention your brain talent when it comes to understanding the workings of situations and events. Now there, I have said what I wanted to say for a long time."

Rachel said, "You have always been a true gentlemen to me and many other people, and it was hard to read between the lines of your true feeling." She said her emotions are still raw because of her husband's death but is getting better with the passing of time and of his gentle understanding.

Thomas reach up and kissed Rachel on the forehead and said to her, "I have strong feeling for you, but I do not want to push too hard because of your healing process in your husband death. You must tell me someday your feeling as I have told you."

A few months later on Sunday morning at church, Rachel approached Thomas and asked Thomas for the afternoon together as the day was a very cold day hovering around the low 40 degrees. Thomas agreed to meet at her farm as soon as he could return his family home in the carriage.

As Thomas was driving toward Rachel's farm, many thoughts cross Thomas's mind: wondering why she ask for this time together. Could it be she's moving back to her homeland in West Virginia, or could it be she is going to tell him this is all that they had together is friendship? Of course, he was bracing himself for the worst.

When arriving at the old farm house and stepped inside, Rachel was standing in the doorway so pretty he could not believe his eyes because she always was one to wear more or less western attire because she was so involved with horses. Her body was slim in way that he had never seen her before. Her eyes were full of glimmer as she greeted him, and their eyes locked onto each other in what seem like an eternity.

Rachel had a roaring warm fire going; it just made everything feel cozy as it shed the cold of the day. Rachel made Thomas feel welcome and comfortable as she started to explain the reason for their time together. She said that it was important that she expresses her feeling in the house where she and her husband started out and wants to put the past behind her because nothing she could do to change the past but looked forward to the future.

"Thomas," she said, "it has been nine months from the time of my husband's passing, but you have been a dedicated friend and someone that I admire and trust. You said to me several months back that I would know when the time comes to express my true feelings. I am totally and deeply in love with you, and those are my feelings."

Thomas looked at her with eye wide open and was truly surprised. It left him speechless for a few seconds. Thomas reached into his pocket and retrieved a small package, as he was opening the package he bent to his knee and said "Rachel will you marry me?" He placed on her ring finger, a ring which belongs to his grandmother Candice. His mother was a wise person and told Thomas you will know when the time is right as she handed the ring to him when leaving for Rachel's house. Rachel was overjoyed with excitement as she was trying to say yes to Thomas.

5
CHAPTER

Beginning of the Third Generation of the Stone Family

Several months passed, and the two were married in the Stone Family home place.

A honeymoon journey for Thomas and Rachel would be to her home state of West Virginia. Rachel's family was not able to attend the wedding because of the distance, but Rachel wanted so much for her family to meet and get to know Thomas. It seems fitting for them to make the trip now, knowing it would be a long time before they could do it again. The next day after the wedding, they were on their way to Charlotte to board the train to Washington and a change in trains bound westward with several stops along the way. The trip would take them almost two days to reach their destination of Wheeling, West Virginia.

Rachel's family was at the train station to greet them, for it had been a long time since her and her family were together. For the next two days, Rachel and her family showed Thomas around the area, and they crossed over the Ohio River by ferry. Thomas wanted to see the black rich soil of the Ohio Amish Country. Thomas was amazed at the farms and how well-maintained they were compared to some of the farms down south.

Of course, the Amish people still wore the traditional dress from yesteryear along with each of the men with very long beards. Thomas was able to talk with several of the Amish people, and each time came away with understanding how nice, and courteous each one was.

They made their way back across the Ohio River once more, and the next day, they were on their way home. Rachel was a person who poured out her love in many different ways for Thomas. She was always complementary toward Thomas and the love that he showed toward her. Thomas said he was a blessed man to have such a wonderful wife. The return trip home was fun and uneventful.

Thomas II was really getting into riding horses in a big way because Rachel was there living in the house, so it was easy for her to spend more time with Thomas II. He was learning things like what some of the names were besides riding horses some were called saddle bred, American saddlehorse, and American saddler, and some were also show horses. He was also learning some medical term like "lordosis" which is similar to human swayback curvature of the spine.

In the meantime, Thomas III was taking a more active role in running the farm. He was into finding better and more efficient ways of milking the cows twice a day because it was so much labor involved, and it was putting a strain on the farm financially. The farm was also growing cotton as their main crops. The nearest cotton gin was located near Lincolnton which was sixteen miles to the northwest, and it was always a hardship on the farmhands to carry the cotton that far for processing. It had to be hauled in several wagons loads which took up much of their time.

One day while talking with his dad, the two of them wanted to explore the possibility of building a cotton gin on the farm, so they could use it and have some of the other farmers in the area to use it as well. After finding out the cost and having people to work the gin, it was not feasible for the investment. So they approached Rachel with the idea of using her farm for the gin and also put in a small country store, so that all the people in the community could use it and it would be closer than the Denver store.

The next step in this planning was meeting with the farmers in the area and asking if they would be willing to co-op the gin and store. Rachel was willing to donate part of her land for this new venture, and this way all the farmer were owners and would use the facilities. Rachel farm was east one and a half mile down 103 and just a wonderful location for all that would use it. It was voted on by a unanimous yes.

The cotton gins are used to process the cotton and separate the seeds from the usable cotton. Most families that were into growing cotton before the invention of the cotton gin had to separate the seeds by hand with many hours of work done in the evening hours after the dinner meals.

Candice and her new husband William Lee Hansard, Lee for short, was just starting on building a new home which would be on the White Oak Farm property, but it would not be in sight of the main house. The whole family was at odds with Candice of her choice of a husband, but of course, it was her decision, and she was deeply in love with this man.

Many months passed and it was proven this man was not worthy of the generosity of the Stone family. It was hard for him to work each day like the others. but when he did work he put his whole body and soul into it and was very talented. Candice, on the other the hand, was hard working and put a lot of enthusiasm into performing well. Candice was equipped with the ability to defuse trouble between Lee and her family and for the most part things went well. Candice and Lee moved into their home, so this was a help in the tension between Lee and Family.

Things at the farm were going well. LeRoy had returned home a couple of times for a visit, and he was a soldier through and through. The riding horses were a big part of the farm as was the milk cows. Thomas III was able to find better ways of milking the cows twice a day. By building long feeding bins as the cows came into the barn and separating the cows with individual stalls to stand in during milking time kept the cows calm.

Thomas III was experimenting with a hand pump that could be attached to each of the cows' four tits for pumping the milk much faster than doing it by hand. The co-op gin was built along with the country store, and the farmers and neighbors were pleased about the new addition to their area.

By now Thomas and Rachel had started their family. Firstborn was Teresa May Stone, and the next was Thomas McCoy Stone IV. Rachel had moved all of her horses over to the White Oak Farm and sold the remaining part of the farm that she and her first husband started several years ago. Rachel job for the farm was the care, breeding, and training of the saddle horses. Of course, this was the love of her life, and she would make good riders of her two children.

Thomas II took ill from a stomach disorder and was not able to recover from the sickness. He died two weeks later and the family was devastated from the loss. He was fifty-six of age. Beforehand, knowing that he may not make it, and with his lawyer's help he turned the farm over into his three children's names. Stock for the farm would go at 55 percent to Thomas III, 35 percent to Candice Diana, and 10 percent to LeRoy because he was not part of the farm.

This was all part of the plan their grandfather had set up before he died in order to keep the farm running and be financially stable. Each of his children was aware of the stock options, and no one contested his will. Now on the other hand, the arrangement did not set well with Lee Hansard, Candice's husband. A meeting was set with the family lawyer, so that Lee could see firsthand that it was all part of long-term planning to keep the farm running within the family.

Candice was the financial person for the farm. But she also did other duties. One day, as Candice was doing some of her duties to keep the barn clean in the hay loft, she discovered a long black snake, and it scared her so bad she lost her balance fell through the opening were the hay was passed through both raising and lowering the hay into the loft.

Needless to say it killed her instantly by landing on her head, neck, and shoulder. When the doctor arrived the only thing he could do was pronounce her dead. Now in the middle of this tragic event, Candice was five months pregnant, and she and her husband were overjoyed with the expectation of a baby. All of the family was having a hard time dealing with their loss. Candice's mother was almost to the point of grieving herself to death because the two were so close after the death of Candice's dad two years earlier.

Two weeks passed after her death, Lee felt like it was time to step up, and announce that he would take over the responsibility of Candice role of doing the finances of the farm. Thomas and his mother said they needed time to think about it for a while before giving him the go ahead.

Thomas said that he needed time to evaluate and familiarize himself with the books and ledger, and that it may take a few weeks because he would need time to work it into his other duties of the farm. Thomas did ask that Lee take up the other duties that Candice had around the farm until they had an answer for him on the book-keeping. Reluctant Lee agreed to their request.

Several weeks passed and Thomas and his Mother Trudy asked Lee to join them for lunch to discuss the bookkeeping of the farm. Trudy lead the conversation by saying that this position of finances is the lifeblood of the farm and business, and the failure to do it correctly would mean hardship for the farm. She went on to say they were aware of his help when Candice was alive and doing the book-keeping, and he had a great deal of knowledge.

They also ask him to keep the other duties that he had already started after Candice's death. As a result of any mishandling or theft would mean an automatic dismissal, and he would be asked to vacate the farm immediately. Thomas went on to say if such time would happen, he would be allowed to take all personal belonging, but the house would stay as part of the family estate; all stock would be rolled back over to the estate as well.

Thomas said to Lee, "We will honor you as long as you honor the family and farm. If you so agree with the teams as we discussed, we will ask you to sign the document that we have asked our lawyer to prepare."

Lee signed the document, and they were on their way to getting the farm back in order after Candice's death.

After a few months had passed, Miss Trudy started to notice that Lee was doing very little of the duties that was expected from him around the farm. So during a meeting between Trudy and Thomas it was decided that it was time for an audit of the books on the farm. Due to the bookkeeping being done there at the farmhouse, Thomas could do the audit of the books late in the evening, so he could avoid any tension between him and Lee.

When Thomas went that evening to open up the small safe where the books were kept, he was not able to unlock the safe because the combination had been changed to another setting which was an absolute no-no. The next day, Thomas and his mother came into the room where Lee was doing his work but waited until the door of the safe was open before going in.

As Thomas stepped inside the room, he walked over in front of the safe, so that Lee could not close the safe's door.

They confronted Lee with his work around the farm, and he said his work on the bookkeeping was taking more of his time, and it was just hard to find the time to get out to his duties there. Thomas asked about the change on the safe lock, his comment was that he wanted to keep the safe from anyone getting into it that should not be in it. Thomas and his mother both said the lock setting was never to be changed without their permission, and that he had not followed procedures as he was instructed.

Miss Trudy spoke up first and said due to his inability to following their instruction correctly they were temporarily suspending his duty as the official bookkeeper for the farm. Thomas made it very clear that he must fulfill his farm duties as it was laid out to him in the beginning and failure to do so would mean immediate removal from the property. Miss Trudy told Lee that the two of them would audit the books, and if they found everything in order they would reinstate him into the job, but it must never happen again.

As Lee was exiting the room both Miss Trudy and Thomas were hard at work looking over the books. They found mistake after mistake as entry errors, math errors, spelling mistakes. It was so bad, and two of them were so confused that it was necessary to call in Rachel for her help. Rachel poured over the books into the wee hours of the morning when she ran across a legal document from a lawyer office in Charlotte called Cannon & Turner Law Firm.

The document showed Candice, and Lee had his name added onto the stock of the farm and it clearly showed in both their names as 35 percent stockholders of the farm. Rachel was too tired to wake Thomas to give him the news, and of course, he needed to sleep. The next morning Thomas and his Mother were told about the finding, and it was such a disappointment because all the stock was to remain in the hands of the family so as to keep the farm financially strong.

Thomas made a change to the combination lock so as no one would be able to open the safe except his Mother and Rachel. Thomas went out to find Lee and asked him to come into house to talk with him and his mother. They once again confronted Lee with their findings and then ordered him off the property. Lee's immediate response was as he put it "I am not going anywhere because I hold 35 percent ownership of the farm." He went on to say that from that day forward he will receive 35 percent of the profits as the money came from the cow's milk, crops, and the saddle horses.

After the family consulted with their lawyer they were told that he is legally bound to the farm with his name on the stock, and the farm must pay him the 35 percent profit from the business. With all that said, the family would expect from Lee a 100 percent working arrangements to earn his fair share and help the farm keep running smoothly. With all that had transpired since Candice's death there was very little positive thinking on the part of the family that Lee would continue working hard to gain a profit for the farm. But one thing for sure, he would never be able to handle the books again.

The two children were growing and Rachel was making good on her desire to make good riders out of both of them and enter them into some riding competition as they get older. Thomas was working hard, and his mother was the official bookkeeper and things were going well and the farm was bringing in some needed profit. Due to Lee being a 35 percent stockholder, he has requested a look at the books to be sure he is receiving his fair share of the profit.

His wish was granted, but it was only fair that someone from the family was there to oversee and watch as he viewed the books. Over the next several months Lee was spending less and less time on his duties as a farmhand, and it was starting to put a strain on the farm financially because more of his duties were being hired out to other workers, of course, he was demanding his 35 percent profit.

Thomas and his mother decided after two years of this non-productivity from Lee. They came up with a plan that could greatly increase their chances of buying out Lee's stock and get rid of him for good. The two of them voted on a stock price for the farm at a market value worth 51 percent under the current value and made Lee an offer of cash money to settle the deal. Lee's house was not part of the settlement because the land was never deeded over to Candice and Lee.

Lee said he would think it over and get back to them in a couple of days. He decided after he was told this was a one-time deal. It was just too good to be true, so he took the settlement and vacated the property the next day after receiving the money. Well, the farm was once again in financially bad shape, but that is what banks are for, and once again Thomas III went to bank in Charlotte to ask for a loan. The farm and family had been through adversities before, and this was not going to stop them this time.

Several years had passed since the buyout of Lee, and the farm was starting to recover from the loan. They needed to stop the bleeding they were getting because of Lee's dishonest ways of conducting business. Rachel was a wonderful mother, and she was doing the teaching of her children the same as Miss Trudy did for her children.

Miss Trudy was trained as teacher, so she was able to help Rachel in the teaching of her grandchildren. By now Miss Trudy was at the age sixty-six years old, and she was starting to show signs of weakness. She was not sure if she could continue on as the farm bookkeeper and asked Thomas and Rachel if Rachel could take over the responsibilities, but first she must be trained.

Rachel agreed and would start right away with the learning process of the bookkeeping. After several months of training, Miss Trudy was showing more signs of weakness, and the only thing she could do at that point was to step back and let Rachel take over the job completely. The whole family was most concerned about her condition and felt like she was not going to make it through the winter months. As the warmer days at the start of spring, Miss Trudy's condition started to turn for the better until she was no longer bedridden. The old country doctor said he had never seen anything like it in these parts.

Teresa was showing all the signs of becoming a pretty young woman and especially when all the good-looking young men started to hang around her during social events and at church. Some of her talents were being very athletic and very competitive especially in the riding of horses. She was well on her way of being in the top of the heap when it came to show horses and competitive riding. She also was hard working around the farm and could in some cases out perform some of the men that worked on the farm.

Well, as all us know, being young and energetic always helped with what we can do and how fast we can do it. She was also showing some sign of interest in the music world and had a wonderful singing voice and joined the church choir. Many of the choir members were elated over the wonderful voice that she had and gave her encouragement to pursue her talent. As Teresa's beautiful voice resonated through some social events, and of course, the church choir she was just happy being a good old country girl and wanted to keep it that way.

Thomas IV was also turning into a young man but still a bit younger than Teresa. He is also showing talent in riding horses. He was like most boys; enjoyed the old fishing pond, just down below the house where he spent many hours with a good friend just taking it easy with a pole in his hands. Thomas was growing up in times were gasoline engines were starting to come on the markets for some farm equipment along with some cars and crude looking trucks to take the place of horse power. Thomas IV was somewhat mechanical-minded and was showing much interest in learning more about gasoline engines and trains and wanted to know more about such devices.

One day, as Thomas IV was outside in the yard and just completing some chores of the day, he heard this colossal of noise going puffing, puffing. He turned around toward the east of route 103 and down the road came what looked like a giant train. It appeared that everyone in the house had heard this thing and came running out to see what was going on.

As Thomas and the others stood there looking at this machine coming into their yard, Thomas III, and Rachel, Miss Trudy came running out the door.

The driver stopped the machine and jumped off and came over to Thomas III and said, "Sir, are you the man of the house?"

And Thomas acknowledge that he was.

The driver said he was Henry Moore II and the representative of Farm Machinery Equipment Company. He said he was there to show his new tractor equipment and asked for his permission to do so.

Mr. Moore took about two hours to show the big tractor and how it can be used as a sawmill to cut logs into lumber as well as plowing the grounds for planting cops. The tractor had four big-steel wheels, so as not to get stuck in the mud during rainy days. They took the tractor out to one of the fields to demonstrate how it could plow the fields for planting. When all was shown about the tractor features then Mr. Moore ask Thomas for an order on the equipment. Thomas said that he would need to think it over before giving a decision on the equipment.

6
CHAPTER

Thomas IV Coming of Age

One day Thomas IV came to his dad and said that he wanted to ride the train from Charlotte to Raleigh, North Carolina, because he was excited about seeing a train for the first time. His dad paused for a few seconds and said to Thomas IV that he knew several people that lived in the Washington, DC, area from his college days. He said that he would send them a telegram and ask if the two of them could come for visit and tour around the big city. Thomas felt like it would give him some time with his son and have a chance for his son to learn about the country and a little bit about politics as well.

Thomas was able to set up the arrangements for the trip, and time was drawing near for them to leave, and both were excited. In the morning of the trip, Rachel had gone out before daybreak to hitch the two horses to the carriage and had everything ready just as dawn was starting to overcome the darkness. So they were underway, at last, of a two-hour ride to the train depot in Charlotte.

It was a nice, clear, cool morning as Teresa sat close to her dad, and all four were wrapped in blankets. The road leads up to the Catawba River at Rozzelle's ferry landing were it crossed over into Mecklenburg County by a ferry drawn by a mule with ropes. On the other side was the Old Plank Road that carried them all the way to the train depot on Trade Street. Thomas told Teresa that going back home she would not be as warm setting next to her mother as setting close beside him going to Charlotte.

When they arrived at the station, the train was still about an hour away, but of course, it was better to be early than late. As they waited for the train they heard from a far distance the chugging of the train coming down the tracks. Not only was Thomas IV excited so was Teresa, she had never seen a train before. As the train pulled into the station father and son boarded the train into the passenger car were in seemed a bit warmer than the outside. Rachel had given them each a warm blanket to snuggle in during their ride. When they sat down in their seats and looked around both noticed a small pop-belly stove in one corner.

Thomas said, "Son, the last time I rode a train, they did not have a stove, and it was hard to stay warm."

The train was passing through towns like Spencer which was a maintenance area for locomotives and it had a turntable for turning the locomotives around to put them into buildings for their maintenance.

The train was making its way northward and was going across the Yadkin river on a very high bridge as Thomas IV was amazed how strong the bridge must be to hold up such a heavyweight train.

Now the train was headed more northeast and toward Raleigh and then into Richmond, Virginia, where the train was delayed for about three hours as crews filled the coal car with coal and filled-up with water to make steam. Another hundred miles to go, and the train was due into Washington around six the next morning. When arriving at Union station, Thomas III's friend Fred Silverman was there to greet them and to take them to his house for a good hot breakfast.

Thomas III was reminiscing to his son about his days of going to college there in Washington and how much of the city was under construction such as the US Capitol Building, Washington Monument, and the Smithsonian Museum. Back in those days, people were able to walk up to the White House, but of course, could not go inside.

The two of them were able to spend time on the mall area between the United States Capitol Building and the Washington

Monument and enjoy the hundreds of people moving about in the city. The ladies were always dressed in their finest outfits matching hats with wide brims, plumes, and of course, those long feathers. Men in their suits with ties, starched callers, and high top hats. They cannot forget about the men with their very thick mustaches which the ladies of the day loved. Thomas IV could not believe his eyes with all the dressed-up people as all seemed to be going in all direction.

Thomas IV said to himself, "Where in the world are all these people going?"

Dress Attire
Men and women of the early Nineteen Hundreds

As the two of them entered the Capitol Building they were able to go inside the balcony area of the House Chamber and witnessed some of the debates that were being discussed on the house floor. Some of the topics were almost like heated debates as each one was trying to get their point across to the other house members. Each one has their own thoughts about how things should be run. As Thomas III pointed out to his son, it is the democratic way of running our government. He went on to point out that each of the men is a representative of each state in each district of the state. No one man has the power to make all the decisions, and it is a collection of ideas and opinions that makes the laws.

In the meantime, Rachel and Teresa had returned home that evening, and as Rachel was stepping off the carriage her foot slid off the footstep and was caught between the spokes of the front wheel and broke her leg in two places. The doctor came and set the leg where it was broken in both places. Rachel did not want to telegraph Thomas on the accident; she decided it would spoil their trip. The doctor gave her strict instructions on the importance of rest during the healing process, and that it would take about six months of recovery time.

It was time for father and son to return home after four wonderful days in Washington. When they arrived at the train station in Charlotte they were looking forward to Rachel being there to greet them with her warm and smiling face. Instead one of the farmhands was there to pick them up and they were told about Rachel's accident, and that she was not able to come. On the ride home, Thomas III was most concerned about Rachel accident, and how it was going to affect her in the coming months. They were all concerned about the well-being of the farm, but they knew that she was a good planner, and that she would figure it out as she has always done.

For the next several months it was a struggle for the family members and the responsibilities had to shift to others as Rachel was recovering. Between Miss Trudy and Rachel they were teaching Teresa the bookkeeping job, and she was catching on fast and doing a good job. Both Thomases were handling the farm duties, and all the jobs were being filled as needed.

Rachel was a good soulmate to Thomas and a wonderful mother to her two children even during the hard times of a broken leg. She was always complementary and encouraging to each of the family members as well as the farmhands and was loved by all. She knew the Lord had blessed her with a special talent of sweetness, and she always wanted to share the talent with others.

Miss Trudy was encouraging Teresa to look at a college to get a teaching degree, so that she would have a profession rather than be a farmhand for rest her life. Miss Trudy had already checked into

Appalachian State College in Boone, North Carolina, for her and received some info concerning a teaching profession. The college was primarily founded for a teachers' college, and it was growing with notoriety from across the state for Western North Carolina Teachers College. One year later, she applied and was accepted and would be heading off in the fall to start her studies.

The White Oak Farm had already established a prestigious name for itself as being one of the leading farms in the Piedmont region of the North Carolina area. George Vanderbilt was in the process of building the Biltmore House Châteauesque-style in Asheville, North Carolina. It was completed in 1895, and the largest house in the US—having thirty-five bedrooms located on 6,950.4 acres or 10.86 square miles.

So in 1895, the Vanderbilt's set out to invite and entertain some of the prominent people in and around the region to establish relationships with neighboring farms so as to learn from each other. Thomas III and Rachel were invited to a four-day events at the Biltmore House with several seminars concerning farming. Much of the time would be spent with entertainment such as polo, horseback riding, some of the country's finest singers and musicians, and a little poker and cigar smoking for the men. Time was set aside for the guess to tour the house for both the men and women. For the men they would tour the farm, gardens, stables, and barns.

For the Stones it was the finest of everything: furniture, bedding, linens, and of course, the decor. But more than anything else, indoor plumbing was the big event in the home. It did give the Stones a chance to get to know some of their distance neighbors, and what they were using in advance technology of the day. One of the neighbors said he bought the big tractor and after learning how everything worked it was now starting to save his farm some money.

Apple farming in and around the region between Bat's Cave and Hendersonville, North Carolina, was becoming some of the county's best and finest apple orchards, for its sweet and tangy taste. Some of the farmers in other areas were investing in the apple orchards knowing it was going to be a booming market as people learned about the orchards and the taste of the apples. Because of the Vanderbilt railroad system, the apple was being ship to much of America larger cities.

As the entertainment ramped up into high gear, Rachel was asked if she would participate in some of the riding events with horses. As Rachel was introduced to her event horse, she pulled the horse over to one side and away from the other horses and riders. She was talking sweetly and gently to the horse named Spike.

She was standing up against the horse trying to bond with the horse in a short period of time. She rubbed the horse's face area and gave Spike some sugar pellets. Rachel inspected the horse legs; his feet and found them to be in good condition. Rachel could sense the horse stallion's status of leadership and knew that she had a good and strong horse in which to work with during the events. Rachel was excited and nervous about the event because it had been a long time since she competed with show horses, but she was determined to do well.

As Rachel took to the arena to perform, she felt her confident start to kick in as she was sitting straight and tall in the saddle. Some of the riding was riding sidesaddle and then jumping back to straddle the horse and walking the horse sideways only to stop and back up the horse gently. Her performance was a hit with the crowd, and she looked as if she was still a young teenage girl while her hair was waving in the wind and glimmering in the sunlight. No one could be more proud and excited than Thomas III. He had not seen her preform that well in years.

Back at the farm, both Teresa and Thomas IV were excited about the return of their parents and wanted to know all about the week, and if their mother had competed in some of the show horse events and how well she did.

During the fall of that year Teresa was readying herself for the trip to Appalachian State College. Many months before she had made out a checklist of things to take and being so well organized that everyone knew she would not leave any items behind. As the day came for Teresa to leave, lo and behold, she was so excited she did leave two suitcases behind and about ten minutes out she realized that she had left the suitcases and had to turn around and go back for them.

It was a good thing that she had to return because her boyfriend for six months, James, was on his way to see her off before leaving. He ran into a problem with his horse and had to find another one to ride. He was just getting there as she and her driver were returning. She was elated to see him and was wondering what had happened to him.

7
CHAPTER

Thomas III Run for Governor

Thomas III was getting a little older and thought perhaps he would look into running for governor of North Carolina because he knew the farmers around the state were not represented well. He knew the farmers were being dictated to when it came to pricing their corps at the wholesale market and wanted to stand up for them with more freedom of free trade. His platform was going to be

- free trade for the farmers, and
- more rights for exporting North Carolina factories' finished good products to other parts of the country and world.

He and Rachel made an exploratory trip to Raleigh and wanted to get to know some of the prominent politicians of the state. His goal was to find out how others would feel about his platform and whether it was worthy of pursuing. Between the tobacco, cotton, and the produced corps it was a large part of the economy for the state and most definitely it was worth fighting for now and into the future. One of the secondary up and coming industry was furniture because of the abundance of trees in the state as the pine tree was king.

Textiles factories were also coming on strong because of the cotton crop in the state. Some of the factories in the northern part of the country were moving to North Carolina because of labor being much cheaper than in the northern states. The railroad and banks were also catching on strong, and it was like a trickledown effect as more and more cotton was grown in the state. Let there be no doubt about it, *Tobacco was king* and it was the largest crop in the state. What the tobacco industry wanted they were away first in line for whatever reason. Tobacco was feeding the banks and the banks were funding the resource for exporting the tobacco.

For Thomas, he was throwing his hat into the arena to run for Governor, and he had many backers from across the state with money to help fund his campaign. Many of the well to do and influential people we're excited about him running for governor and thought he had a very good chance. Thomas and Rachel both hit the campaign trail wide open either by horse and carriage, train, or even on horseback to see the people in the rural areas where trains did not go, or it was hard for a carriage to go through the countryside. Thomas made a comment one day to Rachel that he did not realize how big the state was until they started their campaign movement going back and forth across the state.

On the campaign trail everything was going well and more and more people were getting to know both Thomas and Rachel. They liked what they heard from a most positive and knowledgeable person because first and foremost Thomas was a farmer, and he understood the farmers' point of view. Thomas and Rachel were down in Wilmington, North Carolina, and they were staying next to the Cape Fear river because it was a wonderful and relaxing part of town. Both of them could get some needed rest from being on the campaign trail for so many days and weeks.

As Thomas was getting out of bed, he felt this agonizing pain that hit him all through his lower back, down through both legs, and down into his feet. He was in so much pain it was hard for him to get out of bed. He was bedridden for the rest of the day and was for several days until Rachel decided it was time to take this man home. They traveled back to Raleigh by train and then transferred to another train the next day to Charlotte. While in Raleigh some of Thomas supporters came to greet him and wished him well as he recovers from his illness.

Several months passed, Thomas was still a very sick man with all the pain. The farmhands were much help to Rachel as she needed to move Thomas about the house. Due to Thomas's illness it was decided between the two of them that it was time for Thomas to withdraw and suspend his name form the governor race for this election. Tristful letters were coming in from all part North Carolina concerning his illness and wished him well on his recovery with hope that he would be able to run in the next gubernatorial race in four years.

*****

Thomas IV was coming of age and looking toward his future as a young man. He, of course, was very mechanical-minded and just as his dad did want an opportunity to express his desires. Going to engineering school was somewhat primitive back in his day, but still it was something that he wanted to pursue, and of course, he would someday apply the knowledge to the farm. The University of North Carolina State was offering a degree in the engineering of design of roads and bridges and structure design for buildings. So he was on his way to design school and wanted to prove to himself that he was capable of achieving a degree in engineering.

For Rachel, she was just happy being a wife and mother and still involved in show horses, and the business could not be better for her and the farm. She had hired a man by the name of Steve Baldwin from Tulsa, Oklahoma, which had always been into making hand-carved-crafted leather saddles. Of course, Oklahoma was "cowboy country," and of course, one being into herding cattle had to have the finest of saddles.

He was here because his daughter had moved here with her husband, and the two them had a small business of repairing steam engines for the railroad and some factory-installed steam engines. He wanted to be close to his family and decided to stay in the area.

Someone told him about the White Oak Farm, and he decided to pay a visit on Rachel.

When the man shows Rachel some of his illustrious work, she could not believe her eyes and knew the saddles would be an instance hit with some of her competitive riders. Hand-carved-crafted saddles require several weeks of work, and they would be very expensive. For those who had the money, it was pose no problem, and it did offer a prestigious level of confidence to horse riders as well. The word spread about the hand-carved-crafted saddles and folks from all over the region were coming in to see this man's work, and they all were stunned at what they saw. Many of them had never seen a hand-carved-crafted saddle which included Rachel.

Thomas III was starting to recover from many months of his illness and slowly was moving back into working and running the farm. He was into researching new and better ways of running the farm so as to reduce the overall cost. One of the things that Thomas found during his research was power by water for farms. In addition to mossy creek on the land, there was another small creek that runs through the property near the barn. It was an ideal location to dam the creek and create a small lake, so that a water wheel could be installed to run a small generator to produce electricity.

The electricity would drive pumps for milking the cows; reducing the amount of time during milking twice a day. Not only would it help the farm and the workers, it would be easier for the cows as well, reducing the overall time for the cows standing in the stalls as sometimes they would get agitated from standing so long. After further research on the power by water project, Thomas felt perhaps the technology was still too primitive and decided against the project.

One day, Rachel came to Thomas III and said both kids are in school and away from home. "We need to spend some one-on-one time together. Let's saddle up the horses and ride throughout the farm and enjoy some of the beautiful scenery and spend one or two night under the stars."

Thomas said to Rachel, "Why did it take you so long to come up with such a wonderful idea?"

It was late in the afternoon, and it was decided they would gather their needed supplies and head out the next morning. The next morning was a wonderful, crisp fall day with only high clouds in the sky which would indicate low chance of rain at least for the day. As they set off for their trip with the saddle bags full of supplies, sleeping blankets tied to back of the saddles, and the two of them were like two kids in a candy store; just full of excitement as the farmhands waved them goodbye.

They went to mossy creek and followed the creek bed northward for a little while stopping along the way to rest and water the horses. Thomas decided to wet a hook in the creek to try and catch some lunch. Thomas was skilled at digging for worms; using them for bate. He was in luck as he was able to catch three small basses. Thomas told Rachel to sat back and enjoy the day; that lunch was on him. As they parted from mossy creek they rode along the northern property line and onto an area that was the highest point on the property.

As they stopped and was taking in the scenery from a distance, they could see a large herd of Whitetail deer grazing in the field below. Because Thomas and Rachel were up wind from the deer, the deer were not aware of any possible threat, and they remained calm. From this vantage point they could see the Little Mountain toward the North and the Appalachian Mountain range far in the distance.

From this distance the Appalachian Mountain range looked just like what people have said for years: "the Smoky Mountains" blue in color and smoky. As the two of them started to look for a resting area for the evening and were ready to dismount from the horses they spotted two red foxes chasing what look like several rabbits. It is unusual to see a fox because normally they stay well hidden within the tall grasses or underbrush.

As night time was closing in, the first chore for the evening was to gather firewood because the temperature will dip to mid-forty for the evening. They erected a lean-to in order to capture and reflect some of the heat from the fire. After they finished eating, the night fell into an eerie quietness, as if they were the only two people in the world. The sky was moonlit, still cloudless, and looking at the night sky it was a million stars shining at them.

Thomas was pointing out the big and little dipper for Rachel. Rachel was filling a little chill form the night air and snuggling closer to Thomas as the two them were reminiscing from some of their past both before their marriage and after. They were telling each other how much the Lord had blessed them in their life together as well as their two children and the resources surrounding them.

When they woke up the next morning they could see across the meadow a shiny mist of light fog that made their trip worthwhile with the glimmering beauty of the wonderment of nature at it best. They could hear in the distance the echo sounds of various animals and birds as each was being busy at life. As they were watching, a small herd of deer appeared in the meadow to graze, and it was like Mother Nature just unfolded in front of their eyes. They finished out their day riding to the south and east of the farm and returned home for a good night rest.

Teresa was returning home from college and was eager to reacquaint herself with her family, friends, and especially her boyfriend which she had not seen for several months. Several days later, as she was walking through the hallway, she heard her grandmother Miss Trudy call out as she had fallen trying to step out of bed that morning. The doctor was called in but her injuries were too severe and after several hours later she passed away. Miss Trudy was like a fixture in the household, and it was going to be hard without her support, wisdom, and always her encouragement when doing things, you were not sure about.

Thomas IV was called home from college, and Miss Trudy was buried in the family cemetery which was located on the farm. The cemetery had a knee high wrought iron fence around it and with the arrival of Miss Trudy it was as if the grave plot was filling up fast.

Over time, Teresa was able to find a teaching position in Lincolnton, North Carolina, and ended up moving away once again. But it was something she loved doing and eventually she and her boyfriend were married.

Thomas IV did receive a degree in engineering, and he told his parents that he wanted to explore a few dreams of his own before working at the farm full-time. He did contact the CNO&TP Railroad in Cincinnati, and they hired him to help design some bridges over the Ohio river. Thomas had to move to Cincinnati, and this is where he met a young lady by the named of Virginia Ellen Cain. It was love at first sight as both of them described their first encounter with one another at a church outing on a Sunday afternoon. Virginia was a high society girl coming from a very wealthy family that own a most progressive company of various soap, spices, and some package food produces.

No one could be more down to earth than Virginia as her love and understanding for other people were true and genuine. Her smile made a person feel good about knowing her and enveloped you into her world of beautiful charm. She wanted to work in the family business, but back in those days it was looked down upon for women to work outside the home and especially women of her status. She and her family lived in an area just outside Cincinnati that had some acreage called Indian Hill. They had a grand piano in the home that Virginia was skilled at playing, and she played at several concerts in downtown Cincinnati at the Cincinnati Music Hall as well at church functions.

At about two years into the designing of bridges, Thomas IV was not happy sitting at a design table every day. He was ready to move back home for some good, old-fashioned, downhome cooking and saddled up a horse for some fun in the saddle. Well, for him and Virginia, the moment of truth was upon them as to whether she would marry him and move back to North Carolina to start a family. Thomas purchased a ring and asked Virginia to marry him. He was surprised at her answer. She said to be respectful to her parents told him at the moment she could not accept his proposal as it would be a family matter to discuss with her parents. She did go on to say if it was just her she would say yes, but due to her moving to North Carolina was another thing.

When Thomas told Virginia of his timeline of leaving for North Carolina, she had to set a meeting with her parents. She, of course, wanted to be married at home, and they would need to allow time for the wedding.

As Thomas sits down with her parents, he said to them that he was very much in love with their daughter and was asking for Virginia's hand in marriage, and he had made a decision to move back to North Carolina, so that he could start taking over some of the farm duties and start a family. Well, to his surprise they said it was not their decision, they would support any decision by their daughter, and if she chooses to go to North Carolina that it was just a train ride away.

Two months of planning were underway for the big wedding day. Thomas IV had arranged for his family to ride the CNO&TP Railroad to Cincinnati and arrive one week before the wedding. When his family arrived, John, Carol Cain and family were there to greet them as they stepped off the train. Her parents ware great hosts, and Virginia's dad took Thomas III to visit some of the family factories there in Cincinnati.

The wedding day had arrived; everyone was in place as the wedding began. No one in the Ohio region had ever seen such a grand wedding. The church was full of family and friends as some came as far away as St Louis, Missouri. People from all over Cincinnati were standing outside to see the couple as they exited the church. One big, amazing surprise to all the attendees was the church had a grand piano inside the church. People were whispering as they could not figure out why the grand piano was at the church podium because the church did have a wonderful piano, it was just not a grand piano.

As the organist started to play the *Wedding March*, and Virginia was coming down the aisle. As she got close to the podium she let go of her dad's arm and walked over to the grand piano. She sat down and started to play as if she was in concert at the Cincinnati Music Hall. Many of the people started to cry knowing this would be last to hear her play. As she finishes playing the audience was begging for more which she played two other songs. The wedding finished in grand style and every one outside could not believe their eyes as the wedding couple passed and rode away in a white carriage drawn by two white horses.

A few days later the entire Stone family with Thomas IV's new bride were on the way to North Carolina. The train ride took them to Washington, District of Colombia, which they took a two-day stop over to view the city. Two days later they were on the way home going through Raleigh and then onto Charlotte. Two carriages were at the train station to pick up the Stone family, and one would continue on to Lincolnton to take Teresa and her husband home.

For Virginia, the trip was a wonderful experience, and she was able to see many things that she had never seen before. The newlywed's room was all in new furnishing with a new bed, new chest of draws, and a bureau with fresh linen, and fresh paint on the walls. Both Thomas and Virginia were pleased as they settled into their new surroundings.

Rachel had picked the upstairs' front-left bedroom, so that Virginia would be able view the Appalachian Mountain range far in the distance. On a clear day, one can see the entire range from about Boone and Westward to Back Mountain. A wedding gift from her parent was a new baby grand piano which would be delivered in the next few weeks. The entire family along with the housemaids could not wait on it to be delivered and was looking forward to some good music. Rachel had arranged for Virginia to have a good well-bred horse for a wedding gift with a hand-carved-crafted saddle with her name encrypted on one side, and her home Buckeye state of Ohio on the other side.

Many months had passed things were going good for all the Stone family, but one day Virginia came to the dinner table, and announced that she was really home sick and missed her family more than anyone would ever know. All were saddened about the announcement and each was trying in their own way to comfort her. She was crying and would not eat and finally said that she wanted to return to Ohio for a few weeks visit. Thomas IV told her that he would support her decision to return home, but his duties at the farm would not allow that much time to accompany her. She was fine with his decision and made arrangements to ride the train back to Ohio in a couple of days.

She boarded the train in Charlotte, and she was delighted that she was going home to see her family but knew she would really miss Thomas while away as he was the love of her life. As the train pulled away from the station, and Thomas could no longer see the train as it disappeared around a curve. He was already missing Virginia but knew in his heart that she loved him, as he knew how much he loved her. As always the train runs through Raleigh, Richmond, Virginia and into Washington were she had to change trains on her final leg of her journey to Cincinnati.

Two days after Virginia left the White Oak Farm, the family received a telegram from the Railroad Company. Rachel received it but waited on Thomas IV to return from an afternoon trip to Denver to pick up some supplies. As Thomas open the letter it read:

Mr. Stone,

We want to notify you and your family; there has been a horrible accident involving the train heading into Ohio which your wife Mrs. Virginia Stone was on. A total nineteen people including your wife died. Another thirty people were severely injured and some with minor injuries. One of the passenger cars running off the tracks and went down an embankment of several hundred feet. The accident happens in Pennsylvania near the Ohio river. We believe a rock bolder from a ledge above the tracks rolled down across the tracks impeding the train movement forward and the train engineer could not stop in time to avoid the collection.

With respectfully regrets we are sorry for your family's loss.

Mr. William Keller President
Cincinnati New Orleans &
Texas Pacific Railroad

The next day another telegram arrived to inform them that the Railroad Company had retrieved her body, and it was being forward on to Cincinnati because it was closer than North Carolina. The same day another telegram arrived from the Cains family stating their condolences to Thomas for his loss of Virginia. They were aware of her body being sent to Cincinnati and asked Thomas permission for her remains to be buried in Cincinnati. Due to the train accident it was going to be several weeks before any trains would be able to continue regular's runs. The distance between North Carolina and Cincinnati was too far for him to ride a horse in time for the funeral.

Thomas sent a telegram to the Cain Family requesting a detail letter about the funeral services. He also said that his family was going to have a memorial monument erected to honor her and her name.

Time was passing for Thomas, but it was hard each and every day to forget the memories of Virginia. He kept saying over and over to himself, "How will I ever forget her? She was the love of my life?"

His dad came to him one day to offer some comfort to Thomas IV. He said to him that his life was similar with his relationship with Francesca back when he was in college, but of course, it did not end in tragedy nor were they married. He said he had a hard time dealing with losing Francesca but said also time heals all.

A telegram arrived addressed to Thomas Stone IV from John and Carol Cain's family in Cincinnati, Ohio, and it read:

My wife and I would like to come for a visit to the White Oak Farm and stay for a few days if you and your family would agree to it. We would enjoy seeing where our daughter spent her last days with the man that see loved so much.

A date was set up, and the Cain family were on their way. Thomas IV, Thomas III, and Rachel were in Charlotte at the train station to greet them as they arrived. Mr. Cain said that he wanted to tour the city of Charlotte for it was his first time being in the South and the city. His comments were he did not expect the city to be as large as it is with several high-rise builds in downtown. Thomas said the city is built around farming. The banks were a big part of the industry to help the farmers. Railroad was another large industry because so much of the farming was cotton and cotton had to be shipped to other parts the country.

As they were riding by, Thomas pointed out the United States Mint. Thomas said in addition the other industries; gold was a big part of the economic growth. In 1799, twelve-year-old Conrad Reed pulled a seventeen-pound yellow rock out of Little Meadow Creek in Cabarrus county not far from Charlotte. For the next three years, it made a useful doorstop at the Reed home. His dad later on sold it for $3.50. Hence "gold fever" was born in the region. The United States Mint at Charlotte opened on July 27, 1836.

Mr. Cain said that in the history books of the Revolutionary War, there is much to do over what they called the "Hornets' Nest." He asked Thomas to point out the location. As they rode by the area Thomas pointed out to the Cains the area is now called "the Square" in downtown Charlotte where two main roads intersected Tryon and Trade, but at the time it was the location of the courthouse. The band of loyalist to the US were lying and waiting in and around the courthouse on the British as they arrived in Charlotte. The British were ambushed and did not have a chance for a battle and the only thing they could do was retreat and run for their life. Hence the phrase "Hornets' Nest" was born.

Nicknamed the Queen City, Mrs. Carol Cain wanted to know where the nickname came from as the city of Cincinnati also called the Queen City. Thomas said like its county a few years earlier, Charlotte was named in honor of German princess Charlotte of Mecklenburg Mecklenburg-Strelitz, who had become the Queen Consort of Great Britain and Ireland in 1761, just seven years before the town's incorporation.

By the time the party of five arrived at the farm it was late evening, and Rachel had made their stay in the room across the hall from where Virginia and Thomas room was located. The bedroom door still bore their names because Thomas did not want to remove it. Once Virginia's mother saw the sign on the door she wanted to go inside, and as she stepped into the room tears started running down her face just knowing her daughter was happy there.

The next morning after breakfast, the Cain family was ready to tour the farm as they had never visited such a large farm before. Thomas and Rachel were all too happy to show them around and introduce them to the farmhands as they were proud of each one and their hard work. The farm was very advanced in new technology of the day as Mr. Cain noticed right off. He also noticed how orderly everything was and that everything was in its place. The farm was very clean, and one could tell the farmhands were skilled at their duties and very friendly. Mr. John Cain made the comment that he was picking up on some good pointers that he could apply to his operations in Cincinnati.

Thomas III took them into the barn and showed them the stalls were the cows are milked twice a day. Thomas also pointed out that his vision for the future was automatic milking machines to be installed. The cows were already finished for the morning milking but would be back at 6:00 p.m. and both John and Carol were excited to see the process of milking when they returned. Rachel had them watch one of the trainers going about his business working with a very young horse and getting the horse use to working with people. She explained it is a process with each and every horse and some are harder to work with than others but each will succumb to the training in time.

Rachel was all too excited to show them the stable where the horses are housed during the evening hours along with their grooming time. At the moment they are in the pastures, but as they looked out across the fields they could see some of the horses along with the cows. As Mrs. Carol Cain looked out and was watching the animals grazing she made the comment that it is quiet and peaceful just knowing the animals are doing what they do best.

As they were in the barn Rachel took them over to the area were the handcrafted saddles are made. They were, of course, inspired by the workmanship, and Rachel wanted them to take back home the saddle that was made for Virginia. Mr. and Mrs. Cain did accept the offer.

During lunch, each of the Stone family members joined in to tell how much they enjoyed Virginia and how dedicated Virginia was in her work around the farm. All the farmhands enjoyed working with her as well. When the baby grand piano arrived all the hands wanted to hear her play and play she did and all of them enjoyed her wonderful talent.

Mr. John Cain asked the question, "What is the one thing that has made your family farm so successful?"

Thomas spoke up to say that several things contribute to the farm's longevity but two things that stands out. First after the Civil War and the slaves were free and the farm had hired them as employees. They were starting to make their own money. Thomas II had the vision to make the employees feel a part of business and asked them to join in the decision-making at the weekly meeting. This, of course, was in a rotation bases each week for the employees. Each of the employees was asked to give their opinion of a situation and each had a vote on any situation to move forward or not to move forward.

All of the employees participate in a small profit-sharing plan, one of the earliest plan, in order to give an incentive for them to work smarter and harder. They all share in one thing; "more profit and better working condition." Each employee feels they have a say in the business and, therefore, they guard against wait and each are willing to keep their jobs running smoothly. They ask two things from each employee and that is to always have a willing attitude and to be nice and to be friendly toward their co-workers.

As Thomas was talking, Mr. John Cain was taking notes and will apply some of these skills to his operations back home. The two families spent the rest of the day just sitting and talking and reminiscing about Virginia and her life as both were still trying to cope with her death. One might say it was just good therapy for all.

For the next two days, they spent most of their time together touring the farm on horseback. Mr. and Mrs. Cain had never spent much time riding, and as they found out to be one of the most relaxing event.

Mrs. Cain said, "Time seems to be at a standstill as we were looking at the surrounding beauty of nature."

Thomas asked the Cains about the baby grand piano and what to do with it as no one in the Stone family had any skills at playing it. They both agreed that it should be donated to their church, and they both were sure it would be used a lot over the years.

After several days it was time for the Cains to return to Cincinnati. As they were boarding the train in Charlotte they vowed to return again and asked if Thomas and Rachel would visit them some time in the near future.

8
CHAPTER

Electricity and New Technology

Thomas IV was, like all the pass Thomas Stones, more of the day-to-day operation of the farm was being passed on to him to manage. The time was the early 1900s and a lot of new technology was being developed such as cars, trucks, tractors. And electricity was being brought into factories and some homes. More tracks were being laid throughout the country, and it was eraser to ship the farm's cotton to other parts of the country.

Thomas and his dad decided it was time to purchase two trucks for the farm in order for them to be more efficient and reduce cost. It was decided not to purchase an automobile until the state could do something about the roads. Roads were really poor in around their area especially when they were wet. The roads were like one big muddy mess with large ruts going down on both sides.

The newly formed Electric Power Company was running power-lines down Route 103 and stopped in to see if the farm wanted power for both the home and barn. Of course, that was like music to Stone family's ears, yes, they wanted the power! This is exactly what Thomas III was wanting rather than a gasoline engine to generate electric to power the barn, so they could set up automatic milking machines. Thomas III was true harbinger when comes to new and inventive ways of doing things.

A few days later, here were the men to install the poles to bring in the electricity. So Thomas Sr. and Jr. were on their way to Denver to the farm supply center to see about purchasing automatic milking machines. No one, at the store knew anything about the machines, but someone was due in from their supplier in the next few days, and they would find out from him.

Thomas Sr. said, "Let's go ahead and send a telegraph message so they would be prepared about what we are looking for."

A few minutes later they received a message back stating they would have their represented come to the farm in a couple of days and show the product.

In the meantime, while they were there doing their business, walked in a pretty young woman: slim and trim, very tall, with dark hair not too long and not too short. As she walked in, Thomas Jr. noticed her looking him. She was only in the store for a few minutes and then she was gone. As Thomas and his dad were walking outside to load the wagon this young woman came walking by as if she wanted Thomas to speak to her.

Thomas knotted to her with his hat in his hand and then said hello as she passed by. The two of them finished loading the wagon and headed down the road, but on the way home Thomas asked his dad if he knew her and he did not. Maybe it was someone new in the area. Maybe she was married, so many questions he had and no one to answer them for him.

Several days passed and he kept thinking about this pretty girl and decided to take another trip into Denver knowing very well he would not see her again but maybe someone would know her name and could answer some questions about her. He pulled alongside the Farm Store Center; asked the attendances if anyone knew this lady that was there the same day him and his dad was in the store.

Everybody spoke up said what do you what to know about her? Thomas said well let's start with her name. Nancy Mayfield they said. She comes from a devout Christian family, and she is one of eight children. Her family owns a hundred acre farm several miles north of Denver, and she comes in twice a week to deliver eggs and several other items from the farm.

Of course, he asked if she was married and they said no, but she is somewhat shy and very particular about who she associate herself with. Thomas said what about me; do you think she would like me? Well they said; depends on what type of reputation you have. He wanted to know what day she will be coming back to town again. She does not have a set schedule; it all depends on the hens laying the eggs, they said.

As Thomas started to pull away from the store, he noticed a horse and carriage coming down the road far in distance from the north side of town. He decided to hold up until it arrived in town thinking that it could be the person he was looking for. Sure enough it was Nancy; just the person he wanted to see.

She pulled up and Thomas stepped off his wagon went over to greet her and took her hand and helped her down from the carriage. He introduced himself, and she introduced herself as well. Thomas asks if he could accompany her as she made her rounds in town and she agreed. Thomas told her some things about himself and where his farm was located, and he was just starting to take over more of his dad's responsibilities.

Thomas found out the men at the store were right; she was somewhat shy but very nice and spoke with authority in her voice. After a little while, Thomas asked if he could come to visit her this Saturday to meet her parents and family and go for a ride in the carriage. She accepted his offer and told him to come for lunch that way he could meet the whole family of ten people at the lunch table.

Thomas did keep his appointment with Nancy, and as she promised, the entire family was there to greet him. Her dad asked each of the children to stand and tell a little about themselves along with mother and dad. After each had spoken, her dad asked Thomas to stand and tell a little about himself. As Thomas was speaking he told about his days of working for the railroad in Cincinnati as a design engineer designing bridges that crossed over the Ohio river. He also told about Virginia and his marriage to her and how it ended in tragedy.

As he started to tell the story tears started to swell in his eyes and then started running down his cheeks, and he was at a point he had to stop. He sat down for a minute or two; asked each family member to forgive him that it was a hard thing to do, but that he needed to continue to help get it out of his system. When finished each one came to him to thank him for the story and they we're most humbled by his love for her. Mr. Mayfield wanted a prayer for Thomas before everyone left the table, and then gave his consent for Nancy to go for a ride with Thomas.

The farm was getting the much needed electricity connection, and the man with milking machines was due in the next day. When he arrived, he had several different types depending on a person's budget as to which one would be installed at each stall. Thomas and his son choose the ones that was the medium price range because the machines were not as heavy and they felt like it would be better for the cows. The representative said his company would deliver and install the machine with in the next ten days, and all the farm people responsible for milking are available for instructions on how to use the new machines.

Now time and time again, Thomas was on his way to see Nancy and several months had passed and the love between the two was growing. For Thomas he kept saying, "Can I really love this woman as much as Virginia?" He did have some reservation in his mind about it.

On a bright cool Sunday morning, as Thomas was getting dress for church when he looked out the window, and he could see a sign in the sunlight saying to him; this is the right time to ask Nancy to marry him. Then he started to think of the best way to ask her when the idea came to him because of the closeness of her family that he would at a Sunday luncheon in front of the entire family. But he must first purchase a ring, and around these parts, it was hard to find anyone that would have jewelry for sale. He was able to order a ring from a catalog by telegram but it would take about three weeks to receive it.

The ring arrived and Thomas asked the Mayfield family if he could join them for Sunday lunch. As everyone was finishing up on lunch, Thomas stood up and said he had an announcement to make and as he turned to Nancy, pulled a little box out and open it, and said to Nancy, "Will you marry me?" Instead of Nancy having a chance to respond all the other family members was already saying yes. Eventually they gave Nancy a chance to say yes, and everyone started to celebrate the occasion.

The wedding was planned; it was held in the Baptist Church were the Mayfield's were members. The couple had planned a trip to Asheville, North Carolina, for a honeymoon. New railroad tracks were laid between Charlotte and Asheville, but they could catch the train in Gastonia which was only a few miles away saving them time from having to go to Charlotte.

Thomas and Nancy were on their way as the train zig-zagged through the mountain passes and up the steep terrain toward Asheville. The train was straining as it made its way up the mountain until it reached the somewhat level plateau of a small town called Flat Rock and on into Hendersonville.

A day's ride at best as the train stopped in King's Mountain, Shelby, Tryon, and Hendersonville to pick up passenger and let some off. Nancy was on her first train ride and what a wonderful experience it was for her. She was amazed; looking out the window and seeing train cars either in front or back of them as they rounded the curves in the mountains.

Their honeymoon suite was in the newly constructed Grove Park Inn near downtown Asheville. It was built for the affluent as a golf resort. The designers had in mind meeting and seminars rooms along with an indoor heated swimming pool and spa.

Checking into the room was an adventure in itself with all the people that greeted them. Each of the greeters made them feel welcome; some showed them throughout the lobby area with a fire place big enough to walk into, swimming pool, spa, and the tennis courts. While they were taking the tour, others were taking their luggage to their honeymoon suite. As they made their way into the suite and opened the door, they found an array of knickknacks along with a bottle of Champaign. If one has never been pampered, this was the pinnacle of pampering.

The next morning, a knock on the door and as Thomas opened the door a waiter with a cart full of breakfast food made the morning worthwhile in waking up for. After breakfast they made their way to the spa area and spent several hours just relaxing. In the afternoon it's time to try their luck at tennis since neither had ever played before.

Each evening as they return, they were happy to find in their suite an array items to keep their stomach full. They toured some of the mountain areas with several overlooks and were able to visit the outstanding Biltmore house. They also were able to hike one of the walking trails near the hotel with a wonderful delight of seeing some of the wild birds and other animals.

Once again Rachel had set up the wedding couple's bedroom as she did with Virginia, but this time she put them in one of the side bedrooms, where they could see part the mountain range far in the distance. When they returned home, both Thomas and Nancy were pleased with the room, and especially Nancy because she had to share a room with two other siblings and this bedroom was much larger.

As Nancy was adjusting to her new surroundings, she was not used to the house being so quiet because of her large family. Rachel also made arrangements for a horse to be given as wedding gift. This time on the saddle she had the name of all her sibling carved into both sides and her mother and dad on the very back with fancy letting. Nancy was delighted with her new horse and friend named Lucky. The name was given at birth. Lucky was a reddish-brown stallion with white on each of his feet. Nancy was not experienced at riding a horse and some attention had to be given to her and until she felt comfortable in the saddle.

Many months had passed and the farm was on a steady upturn toward bringing in a good profit, and the farm was growing in the number of farm hands. The milking machines were the talk of the community and many people were stopping by just to see them in action. Nancy was quick at learning some of the new things that was at the White Oak Farm that her family farm was not equipped with.

One of her jobs was to set up the hen houses so the hens were better equipped with laying eggs. The eggs would be used for the farm only and the farmhands. Thomas and Nancy had a standing invitation for Sunday luncheon anytime they wanted to come to the Mayfield house. They would go often, and each time the family wanted to know if she was pregnant yet.

One day, Nancy wanted to know from Thomas more about Virginia because Thomas was not willing to talk about her much. She wanted to know things like what happen to Virginia's horse, the saddle, her personal belongings, which bedroom they shared together. Thomas agreed and said it was time to share some information with her about Virginia. Her horse was sold, the saddle and personal items were sent back on the train to her family in Cincinnati.

For the bedroom, it was the upstairs front-left and much of the furniture was moved out and used in other parts of the house. He also told her Virginia's body was laid to rest in Cincinnati since it would have taken several weeks to send it back to North Carolina because of the repairs needed on the tracks after the accident.

Nancy was aware of the memorial at the grave site but did not know why it was not inside fenced in area. Thomas said that he did not want it inside the fenced area because her body was not there. It was position outside the entrance about twenty-five feet from the gate. A drive circle was made which encircled the entire statue. It was made to look like an angel with a square taper at the bottom all made from marble. The statue was mounted onto a large round granite base. The monument was the first thing you could see as you came upon the grave plot and was a reminder to all of Virginia's outstanding love and devotion to the world that she was a part of.

CHAPTER

Gold Rush and Thomas III's Second Run for Governor

Thomas IV said that it was time to move on from the past, and look to the future with much anticipation for greater things. More and more people were purchasing cars, but the roads were still unpaved. In rural areas, it was hard to get anywhere very fast driving a car. Still the public was fascinated with cars, and it seemed that people could not get enough of seeing a car go by. Some farmers were purchasing tractors, the ones that could afford them, and phasing out using mules to plow the fields. Electricity was growing in popularity throughout all the regions of the country. Small appliances were coming on the market, but electricity was mainly used in homes and businesses for lighting.

The White Oak Farm had a very deep well that was dug by hand many years ago, and it was still delivering good clean cold water to drink. Thomas III wanted to put a hand pump down into the well and put a cover on top of the well. All the farmhand and his son convinced him not too because it was just refreshing to come and draw a good cold bucket of water to quench a thirst on a hot summer's day.

The old well had a rock lining that encircled the entire well from the top all the way to the bottom. These rocks came from the

Dutchman Creek riverbed about two miles away. They were installed during the time of digging to keep the well from caving in on itself and keep the men safe digging the well. As the men placed the rocks, they were tightly packed into each other. They also used cross bracing by using timber to wage across the walls until the digging was completed. As they were digging below the rock level it was not necessary to support below the rock bottom. This information was handed down throughout each generation of the Stone family.

One day as some of the men were digging around the small creek that runs through the property. They were taking out debris that was impeding the flow of water and starting to dam the creek. One of the men saw a shiny object next to creek bank. He bent over and picked it up and though it to be gold. It was about the size of quarter and oblong. He and the other men took it to Thomas Sr., and he decided to take it to Charlotte for assessment of authenticity and value.

Gold was already being mined in and around the area of Charlotte. As it turned out, it was gold they had discovered, and the fever was on to find more. Both Thomas Sr. and Jr. told the men they could look for more gold on the property but only on their own time and weekends. Rules were they must turn in all gold to Thomas Sr., and he would take all to Charlotte to sale. The men would receive 80 percent profit and the farm would receive the other 20 percent. He said he would show them the bill of sale to make sure they were receiving their fair share but it must remain a secret so as not to bring attention to their discovery.

The men and Thomas Jr. were all hard at work looking for the gold all along the river bank. They were panning for gold in the water, and there were talks about starting a small mine in the area where the first nugget was found. Most of the men were not in favor of digging straight down into the ground for fear the ground could collapse on then burying them alive. Each continued to dig along the banks and were finding small amounts of gold as well as the people panning in the stream.

After about a month of looking for gold, the men were anxious about taking it to Assay's Office in Charlotte to find out how much money they have earned. Well, the tally was $7,840, 80 percent for all the men was $6,272, and the farm $1,568. Each of the men received $784 each and it was more than a year's salary. Well, this called for a celebration, but this did not last too long, they we're anxious to get back to work digging for gold being that it was Saturday evening.

Some of the farmhands on Wednesday morning were out in the eastern side of the pasture area repairing some of the rotted fencepost. This is near where the stream come across the pasture and is the same stream that the men were finding gold.

As the men were moving down stream with their work, they discovered several men with picks and shovels digging away and some were in the stream using pan to pan for gold. None of the farmhands said anything to the other men, but one of the men jumped on one of the mules and headed toward the farmhouse.

He started looking for either Thomas Sr. or Jr. and found both together in the barn. He told them what he and the men found as they were working. Thomas Jr. headed for the house to retrieve some rifles as Thomas Sr. saddled the horses. The three men headed toward were they had found the men digging for gold. As they pulled the horses a long side the men that were digging Thomas Sr. said to the men, they were on private property and it was time for them to leave.

The other men shouted back at Thomas and said they a have right to look for gold the same as the White Oak Farm people do. Thomas said no, not on private property. He told them once again it was time for them to vacate the property, or he would have them removed by the law enforcement. The men gather their tools and other items and left the farm.

The mystery question was where did these men find out about the gold? Thomas Sr. said that while he was in the Assay Office in Charlotte a couple men were close by him as he was conducting his business. Maybe someone told them were he was from, and decided to come out to try their luck on looking for gold.

By now, it is probably widespread knowledge about the gold, and they would need to deal with the problems as it comes up. A few days later another group of men were found near the area where the last were seen. Once again they had to be forced off the property.

Soon there were many people surrounding the farm with picks and shovels and gold panning equipment. Most of the men were respectful of the farm and stayed well away from the boundary. Most of the men were not finding any gold and everyone was thinking all the gold was within the farm property.

A couple months later, the men at the farm were out of luck, they were not able to find any more gold. When Thomas returned once more to Charlotte to sale the remaining last bit of gold, he decided to find the geologist there in Charlotte. Thomas asked Mr. George Neal, the geologist, if he would be so kind to visit his farm and try to give some educated reason for the discovery of gold and then it dried up as quickly as it appeared.

Mr. Neal said he would come out middle of next week. He asked Thomas if he and his men could look for an underground spring either on the side of the creek bank or bubbles from beneath the creek's ruining water. Mr. Neal said that it would be in the late afternoon before he would be able to come out and that it would be necessary for him to spend the night and return the next day. Also he asked if they could have several lanterns available. In a couple of days his men were able to find a spring which was about three hundred yards upstream from the area were his men first discovered the gold. So sure enough Mr. Neal was on time late on Wednesday afternoon.

When he arrived they took Mr. Neal straight to the area were they first discovered the gold and to the underground spring. It was getting close to dark, and Mr. Neal asks if they could light the lanterns and hang them on tree limbs over the spring area. As it was getting darker, Mr. Neal started to point out some of glitter that was coming from the spring. There were bunches of it as the lights were shinning on the water.

The men were starting to get excited, gold they said. "gold fever" was starting to set in again. Mr. Neal said no, only fool's gold and mica. Fool's gold is Pyrite: brass-looking mineral that is very brittle and shiny when light strike it. Mica is a crystal material mixed with granite formation. This material will flake off into the underground streams and bubble up as you see it now. Real gold is a soft material and can be shaped with some force without it breaking.

Mr. Neal's theory is that some of the real gold was flaked off from gold vain within the earth's crust. It was forced to the top from the underground steam and was deposited down in the creek bed and along the creek banks. He said, at this point you men, have found most of the gold deposit, but there is gold left in the creek bed but is not worth working yourself to death to find it. The gold that is still remaining will be very small deposits, and it would take a lot of them to make one ounce. Mr. Neal said he would post a note in the Assay Office in Charlotte explaining his finding and that the gold rush was over at the White Oak Farm.

For the Stone family it was a welcome site to see the gold rush was over. It was too much interference with the farm business and some of the men were starting to argue among themselves about the gold. The family and farmhands were very appreciative for Mr. Neal and his expertise concerning the gold. Had it not been for him people would still be looking for gold with many unseen problems.

Rumors were running ramped thought out that Nancy was pregnant with the first baby. She invited all the farm hands into the farm house and told all at one time the rumors were true that she was pregnant. At that Thomas IV was very excited along with the newly going to be grandparents. The next step in this great event was telling her family the wonderful news.

On Sunday, as Thomas and Nancy were having lunch with the Mayfield family, Nancy stood up, pulled her dress tightly around her stomach, and said, "Here it is what you all have been waiting for." For a moment calm and silence came over the family then a burst of joy, laughter, crying filled the room.

Thomas said, "Boy, it a good thing it's not twins, no telling what might happen. I have never seen anything like it."

All the joy and happiness that the family was expressing just made Thomas and Nancy very happy parents to-be.

It has been almost three years since Thomas III made his run for Governor, but due to an illness he had to drop out of the last race. Many of his supporters were almost knotting his door down encouraging him to run. Rachel on the other hand was not so sure. It would mean the two of them would need to hit the campaign trail with very little sleep and riding the train for many hours at a time.

Once again he will put his hat into the ring and try again. The time had come for the two of them to hop aboard the train to Raleigh to renew his acquaintance with his supporters and to raise money for his campaign. As they arrived at the train station in Raleigh and much to their surprise, many people were there to greet them with banners that read: "Our next Governor of North Carolina."

Thomas's platform would be:

1. Farming in this state is our livelihood; exporting our finish goods to other states, and counties are essential to our states growth and economy.
2. Education is top priority: more schools for the rural communities.
3. Paving more roads both in the cities and rural areas.
4. Better trained police force in the cities.
5. Helping the very poor with food and shelter.

Both of them enjoyed campaigning and being in front of large crowds giving a message that both was passionate about. When Thomas would run out of steam then Rachel would take over and tell about her man. She would always point out what a wonderful husband and father he has been over the years. Rachel's speech was always like painting a picture for the audience and it kept the interest of the people all the way to the end.

She told the story about Thomas, and what a wonderful job he's done running the family farm business, and that he was always looking for new and better ways of doing business. She would tell about his decision to bring in electricity to the farm. Then he went to work; finding and having automatic milking machine installed, so that all four tits could be milked at the same time. Now that statement always brought much laughter to the crowd because it was almost unheard-of for a woman to talk about "tits" especially in public.

New train tracks were laid between Raleigh and Fayetteville, so they made their first campaign stop in Fayetteville. They were very surprised at the low turnout of people but pressed on with the campaign speech. Very few people knew the name Thomas Stone III and what he stood for in the communities. Several other stops were much the same, but as he gave his speeches he would always ask the audience to please tell others about what he wanted to do to help the state of North Carolina.

In each community, Thomas and Rachel would visit the local newspaper publisher and ask them to print some of his campaign ideas to help get the message out to the public. The message was getting out: more and more people were showing up for their campaign rallies and it seems much of the residents were excited about his platform.

The residents of North Carolina wanted the state to be recognized as a very progressive state among the United States. After all the state had the coastal areas, with the Outer Banks, Pamlico Sounds, the Piedmont Region, and the long stretch of the Appalachian Mountains, commonly called the Smoky Mountains. All the folks of the state are proud of where they live and worked hard to make it into a great state.

In the Cities of Asheville and Hendersonville it seemed they rolled out the red carpet for Thomas during his campaign stop. Hundreds of people were coming to see him and to hear what he has to say about their state. Thomas would always start his speech with a joke to soften his audience a little.

- "I don't approve of political jokes... I've seen too many of them get elected."
- "Never trust a man when he's in love, drunk, or running for office."

Thomas was reminded once again that the people of western North Carolina always felt a little left out or cutoff from the rest of the state because of their distance from Raleigh. Most of the politicians came from the region of eastern North Carolina, and it seemed the people in the eastern parts of North Carolina were reaping the benefits. They were telling Thomas they were expecting him to change that scenario not that they wanted everything but just to be fair with the system.

It seemed just the opposite when they were campaigning in Wilson. The crowds were large but it seemed everyone was cold toward Thomas and Rachel. Rachel could not stand the suspense of not knowing why people were giving them the cold shoulder, so Rachel pose the question to some of the people standing by. Several spoke up and said you folks come from the Piedmont region. We do not trust people from that region but could not give a definitive answer as to why they did not have any trust. Rachel told Thomas about her findings, and the two of them decided to shakes as many hands and talk to as many as possible.

The next two stops would be in Rocky Mount and Greenville. So the crowds were large again, but this time Thomas and Rachel were spending more time talking to the people opposed to jumping on the platform and starting their speech. It seemed to be working as the audience was more into what they were saying and responding after their speeches. Onward toward New Bern and to Wilmington and again Thomas and Rachel were spending more time getting to know their audience. Each time the people were more open to Thomas and his message.

Arriving back in Raleigh, the two were going to spend the next several days in Raleigh because the election day was just a couple days away. Due to their campaigning tour, the election officials in their county allowed Thomas and Rachel to cast their vote before leaving.

Election day was upon them, and they knew they had worked hard on the campaign trail and now it was up to the voters. As the polls around the state started to close and some of the results were coming in from the Raleigh area things were encouraging, Thomas was leading by a small margin. That was good because Raleigh was in the very heart of eastern North Carolina politician country.

As more of the results were coming in by telegram from different parts of the state, Thomas was still in the lead and still by a small margin. The night was long and into the wee hours of the morning still leading but a much bigger margin. The vote count was still coming in all the way up to night fall of the next day. The news was not good: Thomas had lost the gubernatorial race to the incumbent governor of North Carolina. He lost by approximately 3 percent, and it was heartbreaking to say the least.

Thomas stood in front of his supporters and said, "I worked hard along with my wife Rachel; we did our best, and wanted the best for our state. The people have spoken, and we all must support our governor as we move forward in our endeavor to make our state great."

As Thomas was leaving the platform he reached over to hug and kissed Rachel and thanked her for her hard work.

Back at the farm, once more Thomas told his family and farmhands that his political career was over and that he and Rachel were settling down to be grandparents. During the time Thomas and Rachel were on the campaign trail, little Thomas V was born. Thomas went on to say he wanted the best for the state, but it was not to be. Rachel spoke up and said Thomas's run for the governor offices was fun and exciting but exalting and they were glad it is over. She also said Thomas would have been good for the state because of his ideas and his hard work to implement them.

Early one morning, on one of the coldest day of the year a knock was heard at the front door while the family was eating breakfast. Who could it be at the front door so early? Any of the farmhand would have come through the backdoor without knocking. Thomas IV jumped up and ran to the door. He found a young man standing at the door, and he appeared to be almost frozen to death.

The young man said to Thomas, "Sir, I am here on official business to deliver a massage from Mr. Samuel Cunningham to Mr. Thomas McCoy Stone III and would like to present it to him in person."

Thomas said to come in from the cold and follow him into the kitchen where his father is having breakfast.

The young man presented Thomas with the message and said to Thomas, "Sir, I know nothing of the contents. I am here to deliver the message." He turned and walked from the house.

By this time, you could hear a pin drop. It was so quiet among the family with the suspense of wanting to know what the letter was all about.

Thomas opens the letter very slowly so as not to tear any of the contents. The letter read,

Dear Sir,

I am Samuel Cunningham. I am a business farming entrepreneur located in the Upper State of New York. I am currently looking for a progressive farm in the southern region of the country to purchase, and I am willing to pay top dollar for your farm providing it meets my expectation as I have been told by many people. I will be boarding the train in one week headed south and would like to meet with you in person at your farm in ten days of the receipt of this letter. No answer is necessary as I will be there anyway and will meet others if you are not interested in what I have to say.

The family was stunned about the contents of the letter and could not believe what they were hearing. Thomas said, "Let's not get too excited about the letter, but also let's keep an open mind about the meeting, and see what the man has to offer."

Thomas theory has always been to never shut the door on anything; always hear a man out. Word had already gotten out to the farmhands about Mr. Cunningham coming to the farm and buying out the Stone family. Fear among them were running pretty high and high enough that Thomas had a meeting with them to help settle their nerves. He told them he has no intention of selling the farm, but he is a gentleman enough to hear the man out.

The day came, and as expected Mr. Cunningham arrived with his staff of people. This man was a true gentleman and someone that none of the people at the farm anticipated. Instead of a big black top hat and a nice suite of clothes as they were expecting, he was dressed like someone that just stepped off a machine that was pulled by a team of mules. He bent over and bowed to the people and said he was Samuel Cunningham and wished to speak to Mr. Stone in private if he would be so kind to do so.

Thomas led him to the house and into the business room of the house and closed the door tightly so as not to be interrupted. Mr. Cunningham started to explain his visit and said he has several large farms in New York and that he had been blessed with the knowledge of running the farms, so that it could make sizeable profit for him and his family. He said that he was a Christian man and that he was led to help some of the less fortunate in and around the communities were the farms are located.

He said that he has heard many good reports about the White Oak Farm and that was the reason for his interest. He is looking to move his family south to get away from the brutally cold winters and felt like this would be the ideal location.

Thomas said, "Mr. Cunningham you can run from the cold weather, but there is no escaping from the hot and downright humid weather that we have in the south." He went on to say that he attended school in Washington, DC, where the winters were cold, and at this point he is not sure which is the worst.

The meeting lasted for several hours as the men were getting to know one another: as the two had much in common. As the two men were in their meeting, Thomas IV showed the other men around the farm, and Rachel was excited to show the men the stables and the hand-carved-crafted saddles and how they were made. All the men were overwhelmed with excitement as Steve Baldwin was going about his work on the saddles.

Night time was approaching because of the short days of winter time, and Thomas invited all the men from Mr. Cunningham group to spend the night. They could use one of the unoccupied farmhand houses. Mr. Cunningham thanked Thomas for his offer and said they would stay the night, but they had all of their food and bedding so as not to impose on them during their stay. Mr. Cunningham said he would say goodbye early the next morning.

Mr. Cunningham came to the house just as they were starting to leave and asked Thomas to think over his offer and to give him answer sometime around March 1, and that way it would give both of them an opportunity to think it over. Mr. Cunningham did tell Thomas that he would be talking with other farm in the area but none so appealing as his farm.

The offer was way over anything that Thomas would have ever imagined for the farm and all the holdings. Thomas, Rachel, Thomas IV, and Nancy all sat down together to discuss the offer and what it would mean to the family. Thomas asked each of them not to draw any conclusions until they had a chance to think about it and they would come together again in two weeks and come up with an answer to sell or not to sell.

The day had come to make the decision, and Thomas ask each of them to give their thoughts one-by-one and to take as much time as needed. Rachel started first and her response was an emphatic no as the rest of them followed the same conclusion along with Thomas.

Mr. Cunningham was notified the next day of their decision by Telegraph. The note read:

Dear, Mr. Cunningham

It was a great pleasure meeting you, sir, and what an outstanding personality you possess as a true gentleman. Our entire family has felt that your offer was most generous and something that none of us would have ever imagined.

We have decided to decline your offer as we feel our family is now starting into the fifth generation of the Stone Family and we are strong believers in Family Tradition. We want to honor those that have gone before us, and given this farm a great name and reputation.

Thanks again for your generous offer,
Thomas McCoy Stone III

In the world's news it is been reported rumors of a great war in Europe was breaking out and could possibly draw the United States into it to help our allies. At the end of 1916, the United States started to send troops into Europe but no involvement until 1917. The United States implemented the draft, and Thomas IV was concerned that he may be drafted, but due to him being married and having a child put him in the back of the line unless the war would escalate into a much broader war.

Much of the material being produced in the United States, such as steel, was going toward the war effort and somethings were just hard to get your hands on. Just about all of the war was fought in the muddy trenches along the enemy lines. Not only did they fight the war in the trenches, all the soldiers would eat and sleep in the trenches come rain or shine. The war ended for the Americans in November 1918, and a peace treaty was signed in 1919, and the war was officially over. The total number of military and civilian casualties in World War I was more than 41 million: there were over 18 million deaths and 23 million wounded. Ranking it among the deadliest conflicts in human history. The total number of deaths includes about 11 million military personnel and about 7 million civilians. Death toll for the Americans in World War 1 was 116,516.

Much of the land in and around the battlegrounds was scorched land, and it is hard to believe the land could possibly be rejuvenated by nature to ever look like God's green earth.

This was the Great War to End All Wars they said.

By now many of the homes that had electricity also had radios in the homes, and they we're able to listen to music, big band music, as well a live entertainment such as story hours and dramas. Sports were a big thing as well the news of the day. People were able to listen to the play-by-play of Babe Ruth during the games. The Roaring Twenties was just starting and the skirt's hemlines were rising above the knee level.

The world was entering into the Modern Age of Technology, and it was moving fast and faster than most people could keep up with. It was here to stay; you must rap your arms around it or just move out of the way. Schools and colleges were adding new and exciting courses to their curriculum.

So with all of this going on what does it mean to the White Oak Farms and all the other farms? For farms and all other businesses it will mean they will need to stay ahead of new technology in order to hold down cost. New breeds of tractors were on the market, gone are the days of feeding animals to work the farms. Just feed these new machines with gasoline, and they are good to go for several hours at a time. These tractors could aid in clearing new fields to plant more corps and plow the ground much faster than using mules. More time off for farmers as it cuts back on the numbers hour's farmer must work per day.

The telephone system was being established more for city dwellers rather than the rural areas of the farming communities. More and more outside telephone were being installed in local grocery stores, and this would give access to the rural communities as well.

Switchboard operators were being hired by the thousands. As one old timer put it, "The world is getting smaller by the minute when you can talk to a person across the country." By the end of 1919, 11 million telephones were in homes and businesses.

The time had come for the White Oak Farm to get new technology of its own by installing indoor plumbing: both with running water and toilets. A motorized jet pump was installed inside at the top of the well, and pipes were running underground so as not to freeze during extreme cold weather.

The plumbing system at best was a crude system, but at least they had running water inside the house, and they were able to use the toilet inside. The toilet was a two-piece unit with the water tank mounted near the ceiling with a long chain to pull to the flush valve to operate the toilet. This would allow pressure from up above to carry all the solid waste outside to the septic system. Of course, back in the day no hot water but they could boil the water to take a bath; it sure beat the cold days trying to wash during the winter time on the outside.

Some of the old farmhands were getting older, and it was becoming increasingly hard for some of them to carry on working at the farm. Some of these men had started way back when Thomas II was still living and running the farm. Thomas III told some the men they could live on the farm with their family as long as it was necessary, and that everyone would pitch in to help during their needs. It was gestures like this that help build the wonderful reputation that the Stone family has in the community. Everyone knew the Stone family were people who cared and the willingness to help others.

Even with some of the farmhands getting older, not as many farm hands are needed because of the new machinery to aid in the production of farming.

10
CHAPTER

Bad Weather Ahead

As the Stone family looks toward the future for the farm, and what they need to do to preserve the heritage of the family business for generations to come. Their financial lawyers, as in the past, has recommended they stay with the tradition. Making sure only the ones that will remain on the farm and be the caretakers received the majority of stock in order to keep it financially strong. In the event of one of the caretaker family member decides to move away from the farm then it will be a mandatory ruling to turn over the majority of the farm stock to one's that are still the caretakers.

Thomas and Rachel are happy grandparents and will hope for future additions in the near future in order to strengthen the family.

Though the years Rachel has helped strengthen the farm financially with the horse breeding and selling very well-bred horses along with the handmade and carved saddles. She made sure that her children were good riders and was looking forward to teaching the grandchildren the art of good riders and good horsemanship.

A small town in rural Gaston County
Mount Holly, North Carolina year 1907

On a very warm sunny day, April 19, a gentle breeze was starting to blow from the southwest which was a welcome relief from the
warm humid weather. As the afternoon reached around 2:00 p.m. a
cluster of clouds could be seen from a far distance. The clouds did
give some indication that afternoon storm could be brewing. Just
about an hour later, more evidence of a bad storm was on its way.

Some of the farm hands were starting to come in from the
fields as they could see lightning and hear thunder from the distance.
The family and farmhands were quickly securing items that had the
potential of blowing away during the storm. Rachel and some others
were making sure all the horses were in the stables and the doors to
the stables were secure.

After about forty-five minutes, the storm was really close and
the dark black clouds were just about overhead. Thomas III had one
of the men to sound the alarm by ringing the big farm bell to take
refuge in the storm shelter which was underneath one of the old slave

houses that was nearest to the main house. Over the years the old storm shelter has given refuge many times, and it has proven to be a safe haven for the people as trees have toppled and large limbs have come down and some damage in the wake of the storms.

Just as everyone was safely in the shelter, they could hear the wind starting to pick up and the doors started to vibrate that lead down into the shelter from the outside of the old slave house. Now the rain was starting to fall, and then they could hear hail hitting the doors, and it sounded as if the hail would come through the two cellar doors.

As creatures of habit, everyone was looking up toward the doors as the storm was intensifying. Just a few minutes after the hail begin to fall it started to let up a little; as everyone was thinking the storm was passing.

Then a peaceful quietness fell outside when someone said, "Listen, I hear a sound that sounds like a train." And just about half minute later it was the loudest sound any of them had every head in their lifetime. The noise only lasted about forty-five seconds, and then the wind and rain started to decrease to almost no sound coming from the outside.

After about ten minutes later, the men felt it was safe to open the doors to the cellar and look outside. Everyone was saying it is going to be bad. When they started to open the cellar doors the men could not open them something must be on top keeping them from opening. Several of the men now we're standing on the ladder pushing as hard as they could, and they we're able to open a little. Some of the men standing below decided to change places with men on the ladder, and they pushed one of the doors open enough to allow one small man to pass through. He said that a large part of the slave house had fallen and was blocking the doors. He was able to pull most of the debris to one side, allowing the one door to open so others could free themselves of the cellar. As more of the men were able to get outside they were able to free the doors of the debris, so that everyone could come outside.

Some of the women started to cry as they looked around and could see the destruction all around. Most of the stable's roof was gone and leaving all the horses standing in the stalls, but thank goodness, none were injured. Two of the pigs were killed by flying debris and several were injured. Not a trace of the hen houses that Nancy worked on so hard to organize and build. Many of the hens were scattered on the farm, but many were killed during the storm.

Most all the cattle were sent out to pasture before the storm knowing that was the safest place for the cattle. The two old outhouses were totally gone; another old slave house was totally destroyed along with the old slave house where the cellar was underneath it. Luckily the old farmhouse was in good condition only minor repairs would be required. Debris was scattered about in many different direction, and it was going to require weeks of work just to clean up the debris and get it looking like a farm once again.

The Stone family said they would come up with a plan of action as how best to start with the recovery efforts and would like for everyone to meet back at the farm around noon tomorrow.

As each of them came together the next day. Thomas said to each, "We must be thankful to the Lord that he allowed each of us to ride out the storm without any physical harm to any of us. From what we have been told by the sheriff, the White Oak Farm was hit the hardest during the storm. He said the tornado cut a path of destruction approximately one mile shearing off trees at about a twenty feet above ground level. The width was approximately three hundred feet wide."

The reverend, Willie Moore, was there during the gathering. Thomas asked the minister to say a prayer for their lives being spared during the storm. Each of them held hands as the prayer was being said.

Thomas said they would start by building back the stables for the horses but would only use a few men to do so. He said the women could help in the cleanup effort around the grounds and put the debris in piles around the farm, so that it could be burned at a later time. His main concern was to keep the farm running and being productive during the cleanup efforts, otherwise it would be costly to the farm.

As Thomas was finishing up his instructions to the farmhands the Reverend Willie Moore stood up and told Thomas that the church has offered their help in building back some of the structures that have been damaged during the tornado. He said it was neighbors helping neighbors in time of need. He also said that the White Oak Farm has done a lot to help the community over the years, and it was time for the community to help the White Oak Farm.

Nancy's family was there during the meeting, and the family was there to help in any way they could. Mr. Mayfield, Nancy's father, said he had spoken to their church and many of the members were willing help as well.

As work began to put the farm back together, Thomas was able to keep work on going for the farm business so as not to lose production. The men coming in from the church brought their wives with them to help in the ground cleanup and for the noonday meals.

Within two weeks, most of the stable was repaired and most of the debris from the ground was picked up. The debris was put into twenty different piles to be burned sometime in the fall as the weather turns cooler and damp so as not to start a fire on the property. As the work came to an end for the church people, both Thomas Sr. and Thomas Jr. asked the people to gather around for a word of thanks for their hard work.

Thomas Sr. said, "Once again let's pray for our blessing and hard work but most of all our love for one another. Thomas and Rachel made a point to shake the hands of each person that had helped and worked so hard during their time of need. Thomas told the people that their need was great and overwhelming but the strongest and most rewarding part of their need was the bonding of closeness to each other. With that he said a big thank you to all and ended with a "God bless our people and community."

Several months had passed since the tornado passed through the farm, and the daily routine of life was getting back to normal for the farm. The Stone family made sure the old storm shelter was repaired and cleaned out so if it was needed again people would feel comfortable going inside.

They were smart people; they made a checklist of things to be updated twice a year to make sure everyone would know what to do during an emergency. The old slave house was totally removed that was over the storm shelter and replaced with a covered area for staging the production of farm products. The cover would help in keeping the storm cellar dry during heavy rain because the water would trickle through the ground into the cellar.

CHAPTER

Thomas III Run for United States Senate

One day Thomas III asked Rachel to set aside some time to talk with him about a subject he had been thinking about for a long time after the tornado. The time was set aside as Thomas began to talk. He said to her that he was so overwhelmed by the generosity of the people that helped during the tornado crisis of the farm that he wanted to give back to the community.

Rachel, in her mind, had already figured out what was on Thomas mind. He went on to say that his run for governor of North Carolina did not prove to be successful: either time and was looking at running for the US Senate as one of the seats would be up for election next year. Thomas talked for a while longer and then ask Rachel her thoughts on the matter.

Rachel explained that she knew what was on his mind before sitting down because she knew that he was in deep thought from time to time. She had observed Thomas during the campaigning run for governor, and his mannerism was much the same. Rachel said she would support any decision that he made, and she would be by his side all the way win or lose. She said she knew his heart was into helping the farmers of the state of North Carolina, and this venture maybe would prove to be better than being governor.

The next step in the process is filing by January 1 of next year, and he has the right credentials for registering as a candidate for the US Senate. Once all the right paperwork is completed then he can start to campaign in the state.

His platform will be as follows:

1. To help the farmers in the state of North Carolina as well as all farmers in the country.
    a. Exporting farmer product to other states and countries.
    b. Regulating the amount a farmer can grow per acre of any one crop, in order to maintain a balance so as to keep prices stable.
2. Roads
    a. This country is seeing a boom in manufacturing automobile and there are not enough good roads to support the demand for vehicles.
    b. Building bridges instead of relying on ferries to cross over rivers and creeks or bodies of water.
3. Helping the very poor and disables
    a. Helping with housing and meals
    b. Helping with medical cost.
4. Providing Jobs for the state
    a. Bring in new industry into the state to provide jobs for the city's residents.
    b. Provide better water and sewer for the cities.

After all the right credentials were in placed, it was time for Thomas and Rachel to hit the campaign trail once again. This time things were different because Thomas was well-known compared to his opponent and there was no divide between east and west of the state as in the governor race. As Thomas and Rachel made their campaign stops most of the people were warm and friendly and people were supporters of Thomas's platform. Most folks were sympathizers of the farmers and their mistreatment by the state and federal government.

Thomas and Rachel were both upbeat and excited about the campaign. They were out among the people shaking hands as most people were positive about the possible fresh new blood to represent the state in the Halls of Senate. This time around, Rachel took more of a backseat role in the campaign because the people knew Thomas and what he stood for and both felt it was in Thomas's best interest. Thomas was fortunate to have the financial backing from so many people around the state.

Time was drawing near for election day, and the entire family decided to go to Charlotte were Thomas's election headquarters was located. The day had finally arrived, but it would be after 7:00 p.m. before any news would come in about the election. At last, some news was starting to trickle in and it was all good news: Thomas was leading by a large margin.

Of course, it is too early to get too excited about the news. Each hour the news was the same until around 4:00 a.m. it was obvious Thomas would be the next state of North Carolina Senator. Much celebration was in order for the entire family, and finally, the family was able to get to bed by 7:00 a.m., but it was a short rest because the news media and his supporters were anxious—wanting to hear from Thomas.

As Thomas stood in front of his supporters, he thanked all that worked so hard and tireless during the campaign. He said he would return the hard work by working for them and for the state of North Carolina and America to build a better country. He went on to say that he has some mighty big shoes to fill because his grandfather was a United States Senator from North Carolina. He is committed to be a good and honest US Senator like his grandfather.

Late in the afternoon the family was able to leave Charlotte for the short trip back to the farm. Everyone was asleep just a couple miles down the road except for Thomas—he was just too excited to sleep, and his mind was going a mile a minute as to what he wanted to achieve in his first hundred days in office.

As they arrived back at the farm, all the farmhands came running out to greet them, and all were overjoyed with excitement for winning the election. All were saying, "Tell us about the election, and when will you go to Washington."

Thomas thanked each of them for their support along with their hard work to make it possible to run for public office. He said once the term limit is over for the outgoing senator at the first of the year he will be sworn into office. He also said that he and Rachel will need to look for a home in Washington because about three quarter of his time will be spent in the Washington area.

As luck would have it Nancy became pregnant with the second baby as Thomas and Rachel were making preparation to leave for Washington to look for a house. As it was the last time, when Thomas V was born, Thomas and Rachel were on the campaigning trail for Governor. Of course, the grandparents were delighted about the announcement and would look forward to the new arrival of the family.

Once again Thomas IV and Nancy were the drivers for his parents to the train station in Charlotte. As they arrived at the train station Thomas IV could tell right away there was some trains on the tracks that he had not seen before since his days of working for the railroad. Thomas IV was so excited about the new train equipment, he almost forgot to say goodbye to his parents.

When Thomas and Rachel arrived in Washington, to meet them were a few of Thomas's constituents from Congress and their wives to greet them. It was very late in the afternoon and the party of ten headed for dinner at popular hangout restaurant for the members of Congress very near the capitol building. Well, as expected, Thomas was so excited, the only thing he could do was ask many questions about the procedures of Congress.

As the group took Thomas and Rachel to the hotel, they gave pointers as to where to look for houses that would be convenient to the offices of Congress. In a couple of days, they were able to find just what they were hoping for: it was a rental house fully-furnished, but Rachel said it had to be thoroughly cleaned before moving in. Before leaving town and going back home, the lease agreement was signed and a cleaning company was found to do the work.

In three weeks the couple would return with all their personal belongings to get settle into their new surroundings. Thomas told Rachel he could not wait for the orientation for the new members of Senate, so that he could get on with his journey to be a Senator. Rachel said she was looking forward to getting to know many of the wives and would start that the next day because she had already been invited for lunch. Thomas already had much of what he needed to set up his office, and he would have that done the very first day. The next day he would meet with his staff of people and get to know them and they would get to know him as well.

As Thomas and Rachel were settling into Washington, it was business as usual on the farm and once again the duties fell into the hands of Thomas IV and Nancy to keep everything running smooth. Almost two years to the date of the tornado, the skies started to open into a horrific downpour of rain and more rain. For about six and half days it rained very hard leaving all the creeks swollen above the creek banks.

Several of the old timer farmhands begin to report to Thomas that they were in fear of flooding throughout the farm from the mossy creek. Of course, the creek was a large creek and most of the water is feed by the mountains' run off. The old timers from past experience believed the flood would come within twenty-four hours, and the farm should prepare for it the best they could.

Thomas immediately telephoned his dad in Washington and reported to him what had transpired in the last six days with the rain and what the old timers were telling him about a possible flood on the farm and surrounding areas. His dad agreed and said take heed to the warning. In the late afternoon, sure enough some of the men near the Mossy Creek saw the water starting to rise, and it was coming so fast they could hardly get out of way of the running water. They were able to sound the alarm that the flood water was on the way and everyone should get to higher ground.

They were able to reach an area which is approximately seventy-five to one hundred feet above the farm level, and it should keep them safe and dry. When everyone had reached the safe area and as they looked back, they could see the flood water rising on the farm. Thomas gave thanks to the men that had knowledge enough to give the warning. As darkness fell upon the area it was clear at least one night would be spent outside the farm. Into the wooded area they did stay the night and being prepared was making sure food and water was all part of their preparations.

With the beginning of daybreak they were able to see the flood-water was no longer rising. They also could see the water up to the ridge they were on. Thomas and one of the farmhands decided to check out the depth of the water and found it to be about two feet. It was decided to wait until late in the afternoon to try any attempt to return to the farm.

At about 3:00 p.m., it was time to attempt the return to the farm, and at that point it was about ankle deep, and they could see where they were walking so as not to drop off into any low areas. They could see some damage from the flood but it was not extensive. The two remaining slave houses water came in about twelve inches, and they would need to be dried out before the men could go back in for living quarters. The storm cellar was completely flooded. All the chicken were roosting, the pigs were able to keep their heads above water, and of course, the stables were flooded, but the horses and cattle were all sent out to pasture before the flood.

Within several hours, all the water was down except for low areas. Two men were sent out to check on some other areas of the farm and found the dam was breached at the pond. The pond was put in place many years ago to hold water back for the pond, so as to water the livestock. This was in the small creek that ran alongside the farm and provided the pond with water. The pond made it easy for the livestock to drink from the pond as the creek bed was too deep for them to drink from.

Thomas called his dad to let him know about the flood, and they were in the process of accessing damage. He told his dad about the storm cellar being flooded and asked his advice on how best to remove the water. His dad said to use the jet pump they had on hand as a backup unit for the well. A day and half the cellar was drained.

Several months passed and things were not going well for the care of the horses, and it was time to call Rachel home and get things on the right track again. Once Rachel returned home she could see right off many of the problems, and she was sure to make things right again. She notified Thomas that it was imperative to remain home for several months and train someone in the care of the horses because the horses are a big part of the farm business.

As it turned out, Rachel could see that no one could care for the horses like her. Time would need to be shared between Washington and the farm as long as Thomas agreed. Thomas was so in love with Rachel that he could hardly bare being without her for long periods of time, but of course, the Senate was his calling, and he would need to endure.

At last the day had come, the new addition to the family arrived—Mary Elizabeth Stone. What a great joy it was for Rachel to be home to witness the birth of her granddaughter. She told everyone the minute this child can sit up she will set on a horse. That was Rachel's way of showing her excitement, of course, she already had Thomas V riding, and he loved riding at four years old.

As the years passed, Thomas III was becoming a senior leader in the Senate and was a well-respected Senator both in Congress as well in the State of North Carolina. Rachel was still toggling her time back and forth between Washington and the farm.

As both kids were growing up, their mother Nancy made sure that both got a good education, and they made good grades during the process. Many times during the years both kids would accompany their grandmother Rachel to Washington and spend times with her and Thomas and would often visit the US Capitol Building and just have fun playing on the Mall Area between the Capitol and the Washington Monument.

Both were able to learn much about the history of our country and how important it is to preserve the freedom that each of us enjoy as citizens. Part of their years of growing up was during the depression, and they were able to see firsthand the hardships that many American were faced with by spending time in Washington.

Times became hard for the farm during the depression as people were not able to buy as much from the farmers as in the past. Some of the workers were laid off as they were no longer needed, and of course, some of the worker became bitter about the laying off, but it was the way of life.

"Depression Years and how hard it was to survive".

Some of the stories coming from the depression era were horrifying as people were trying to survive through such deplorable conditions.

One such story was a family living in Mecklenburg County on a dirt country road between Suffletown and Long Creek in old farmhouse. This family moved there from the city as they could no longer afford the house in the city. The father had found a part-time job at a nearby mill. The pay was enough to pay for the rent and to buy some food essentials such as flour and potatoes.

On a very hot summer day a knock on the door was heard by the mother, and as she entered the hallway of the door entrance she could see a large family standing at the door: a father and mother and four small kids.

The mother opens the door and the father said to her, "Mam, we all are very hungry and have not eaten in two days. Could you be so kind and share a little food?"

She looked down at the kids and said we only have flour for making biscuits and a little sugar to sprinkle on top. She went on to say they have no meat and all the potatoes have been eaten, and as she was talking, she was already into making biscuits for the family.

As soon as the biscuits were taken from the oven and handed out to each, they were looking for more. The mother told them she would need to save the rest for her family as they were in need as well. The mother watched the family leave going down the road walking and each had their own little sack of clothing. The mother was waving goodbye with tears running down her face for she knew that was all that she could do to help the family.

Rachel was making good on her promise to make good riders out of both grandchildren. She was also showing them how to care for the horses and how to love and respect them. Rachel was almost always at home when the two grandchildren were in riding competition, so she could coach each one during the events. Both grandchildren were growing, and Thomas had already chosen and been accepted by North Carolina State University; he wanted to major in Horticulture.

12
CHAPTER

Old Friendships Never Die

Thomas III was working in his office one afternoon with a deadline looming for some new legislation concerning the military. This legislation was top secret due to a huge build-up in military personnel. The United States could already sense deterioration in relationship between the United States and Japan. Not only was there concerns about Japan, Germany was on the move in Europe and starting to take over some of the small European countries.

As Thomas was deep in thought the telephone rang from his secretary, and her voice carried a message saying that a lady by the name of Francesca was on the line, and she wishes to speak with him. As Thomas picked up the telephone; Francesca's voice was like a breath of fresh air that started Thomas heart to beat fast, and at a point he could hardly speak.

Fran explained she and her two children were in Washington for sightseeing adventures and wanted to call because she knew he was a Senator. They talked for a little while, and Thomas told her he did not want to be rude, but he was under a most important legislative deadline but would like to meet up with her and her children for a meal. It was decided breakfast the next morning would fit his schedule best because he was due on the Senate floor at 1:00 p.m.

As planned, Fran and her family was there waiting on Thomas as he entered the restaurant. Of course, both had aged as she was able to recognize Thomas from some of the photographs that have been in the newspapers from time to time. Fran introduced her children as Antonio and Anna Armando and both are college students. She went on to explain that she had married a man by the name of Gino Armando of Italian decent.

His father started a small newspaper business, and as Gino started into the business his goal was to grow the business and make into a large newspaper in the local area. Gino was very aggressive and wanted to do a lot in the field as far as covering different news items. He was in New York City on a very damp and cold day covering the city workers' protest against the New York City pay scale. Gino came down with pneumonia and died about two weeks later, and this was four years ago.

Many years back, she and her siblings sold the bakery to a brother after her mother's death and he has transformed it into a very large and vibrant bakery.

Fran's plans for the future will be for her two children to take over the newspaper business as soon as they complete their college education. Due to her husband's death she had to step in to oversee the business, but she is not happy with the new responsibilities and looking forward to day that she will be free of the duties.

Fran wanted to know all about Thomas's life, and he did give her details about his life and the lady that he married. He told her about the two runs for governor of the state of North Carolina but was unsuccessful in his venture. He went on to tell her about the disappearance of Lily, his granddaughter. Fran had kept up with the story in the newspaper, and that she was aware of the abduction.

It was a good meeting between the two, and they parted ways by saying they would get together again, and Thomas wanted Fran to meet Rachel.

13
CHAPTER

Thomas Mccoy Stone III
Scandal that Rocked the Halls of
Congress in Washington, DC

A letter arrived one day, addressed to Thomas McCoy Stone III.
The return address was Standard Oil Company Cleveland, Ohio.
Rachel was at home at the time, and she called to ask Thomas's permission to open the letter not knowing if it could be official business
of the United States Government. Permission was given and as she
opened the letter she began to read the contents to Thomas.

Dear Mr. Stone,

Our company of Standard Oil formed a
team of geologists working in the area of your
farm, but not on your farm property, have reason
to believe oil could be found on your property
or near it. We would like to send the same team
of geologist to investigate any such finding. The
team of geologists are experts in their field and
would know where to look without any interrup-

tion to the daily routine of your farm and the people that run it.

We would like to ask for permission to do so and at a convenient time in which to come. Any such finding would belong to your farm for all mineral rights are the holding of the property owner.

Please advise us by letter or telegram

Sincerely,
Charles Goodwin V.P of Research
Standard Oil Company
Research Drive
Cleveland, Ohio

Thomas paused for a few seconds as he gathered his thoughts and then advised Rachel to turn over all decisions to Thomas IV, and that he would back any decision made by his son Thomas.

Rachel showed the letter to her son and said that she had spoken with his dad about the matter. He wanted you to handle and he would back any decision that you make.

Thomas took about a week before he came to any decision and, in the meantime, done some research on extracting oil from the ground. He then sent a telegram to the headquarters of Standard Oil that he would allow the team of geologist to visit the farm and a person from the farm would accompany them during their research.

When the geologists arrived, they met with Thomas and showed him some of the equipment used in their research. They explained that during their research offsite of the farm, they had found small amount of oil in the mossy creek downstream as it exited the White Oak Farm. They went on to say that an older gentleman had advised Standard Oil that he had notice small black balls of oil floating down the Mossy Creek that runs through his farm about two miles downstream from the White Oak Farm. They were able to trace the oil deposit up to the property line at which time the letter was written for permission to continue with the research.

After several days of research and study the geologist came to the conclusion and what they found to be was crude oil. It was definitely coming from area about one-quarter mile into the White Oak Farm, and down-ways from the cave area where the slaves took refuge during the Civil War. It was not the creek bed but was located about one hundred yards from the creek. The oil was coming through the surface and was running downhill into the creek.

The geologists were concerned about the impact on the environment and getting oil into the drinking water as it runs into larger bodies of waters and rivers. Their recommendations were to have Standard Oil do exploratory drilling several hundred feet down to find out if there is any content of crude oil reservoir deposits beneath the surface.

They told Thomas that any such action on the part of Standard Oil would need to be legally documented and signed by both parties, and it could take up to six months and up to a year to have all the right documents and equipment in place. They left the area with the notion that someone from corporate office would be in touch and explained all the procedures to get started.

About month later, someone from the corporate office called to inform Thomas that a person from the legal department would meet with him in one week if he would be available. They were not sure which person would meet with him because of their tight schedule. The day came for the person to meet with Thomas, and the man's name was Jess Turner, and he was on time.

Jess laid out all the legal documents and explained to Thomas what each one represented. He explained that, of course, the minerals were owned by the White Oak Farm. If they should discover oil, the breakdown of payment of each party would be as noted; 65 percent for Standard Oil because they are the ones who put up all the upfront money, all the equipment, manpower, permits, storage, hauling of the product, and clean up; 35 percent to the White Oak Farm. He went on to say it doesn't seem fair but one must understand the farm will not suffer any financial lost if oil is not discovered.

Jess instructed Thomas to look over the documents and have his lawyer to look them over as well before signing. If they feel that everything is in order, sign and send to the appropriate address listed on the cover letter. Jess reiterated the process could take six months and up to a year before the work could start depending on the schedule of well digging units.

Jess left the farm, and Thomas put a call into his dad in Washington to fill him in and get his opinion. Several weeks later, as Rachel was in Washington starting to read the morning newspaper; the headline of the day was, "Prominent Senator from North Carolina in Collusion with Standard Oil Company." How and where did anyone get any information of that sort was a puzzle to all that knew Thomas III. There was much said in the article but most was taken out context and some was just an out and out lies to tell the truth.

Thomas was being accused of taking special privilege from Standard Oil by drilling for oil on his property in exchange for voting in favor of the large and rich oil companies. What a mess this has turned into in our great Capitol of Washington, DC. For several weeks that was the talk of the town. Many of Thomas's colleagues were coming to Thomas's office and advising him to do something to put a stop to this nonsense.

Thomas decided to go for broke with the news media as he was going to publish the information that he has presented on the floor of the Senate as to reason for all of this madness. He handed over the letter that was mailed to him at his home in North Carolina along with the minutes of the meeting with the geologist that visited with his son at the farm. He also handed over the legal documents from the meeting with Jess Turner. The documents had not been signed at this point.

When the newspapers hit the door steps and newsstands around the country it almost blew the socks off the people that were reading the paper. At that point they knew much of what they have been reading was a hoax.

Needless to say Thomas IV was able to contact the Standard Oil people to let them know his decision with the oil contract for the White Oak Farm. Of course, it was a no-go but the Standard Oil people were expecting the call in lieu of all the bad publicity. They did tell Thomas. Standard Oil will come out to find a way to cap the oil that is getting into the mossy creek to keep the environment safe.

Thomas III was so disturbed about the allegation of such scandalous behavior that he wanted to get to the bottom of this at any cost. He hired a private detective to start researching how this would have gotten out to the public and how it ended up in the newspapers. The private detective named Rusty Johnson started to interview Thomas's office staff, his secretary, and all the cleaning and maintenance personnel.

Mr. Johnson had worked on this for several weeks, and it seems to go nowhere. He then turned his attention to the White Oak Farm. His thinking was maybe someone from the farm had a motive for getting even with the farm over some grievance. So Mr. Johnson decided it was time for a trip to North Carolina. He interviewed each person in the household and all the farmhands because each of them knew about the visit of Standard Oil company. He, being a very good detective, could not pick up on any mistrust from anyone and headed back to Washington.

As Mr. Johnson was pondering over his notes, he came across something that looked suspicious during an interview with one of the cleaning personnel. The lady said that her husband came early to pick her up and passing the time away was setting at the secretary's desk. Mr. Johnson decided it was time for another interview with this lady and her husband. Mr. Johnson reported his findings to the Washington Police Department and felt like it was worthy of a warrant to bring her and her husband in for an interview but this time on a professional level. The police granted the warrant and went out to bring in the wife and husband.

During the interview with the husband, Mr. Johnson and the police officer noticed an unusual nervousness on the husband's part. So much so that the man was sweating to the point his shirt was becoming wet. They could smell a rat and kept pounding on the man, and he finally broke down and revealed what happened the night he went to pick up his wife.

As he was sitting in the office chair of the secretary, in the trash can he found several discarded papers. He decided to read some of them, and the info of the Standard Oil Company was part of the reading. He then decided to take the typewritten letters home and figured it would be a gold mine in the making. Naturally the newspapers are looking for high-profile stories to print and certainly this is one of them.

Thomas had dictated several letters about his discussions with his son Thomas IV in order to keep a running record of the dealings with Standard Oil Company in the event they were not on the level with honesty. The secretary had started over several times as she was trying to be as perfect as possible with Thomas writing's and that was where the discarded letters were coming from.

The man was charged with stolen property, starting a misleading story, and falsifying rumors about a prominent US Senator. The man was tried and convicted of all three count of conspiracy and received a three-year jail sentence.

Thomas invited the press into his office for a press conference concerning him and the Standard Oil Company. He told them to put the subject to rest and left the room.

14

CHAPTER

Thomas V's Tour across the Country and Alaska Plus a Surprise for the Stone Family

After graduation from college with a degree in horticulture, Thomas V returned home and was eager to get started. But it was not at the farm. He asked for a meeting with his parents and explained to them he was like his grandfather and dad: he has a few wild oaks to sow before settling down to the daily routine of farm duties.

From a small child he had a desire to travel the United States and see the countryside and especially now that he has studied farmland in different areas of the country. But his one big desire is to see Alaska. He has asked for a year for his tour of the country and Alaska before settling down on the farm. He went on to say with so many railroad tracks crossing the country, that it would be easy to travel. He would fund his trip by having layovers in different towns and cities working at small jobs. When reaching Seattle, Washington, and with a layover there his plan is to fly to Alaska and return to the farm in North Carolina by airplane.

His dad and mother both agreed. They would honor his desires and wish him Godspeed with his endeavor. The one thing they ask for would be regular updates on his whereabouts either by letter or a phone call from time to time. Money was no problem if he needed it so don't hesitate to ask: they want him safe.

A week later Thomas V was taken to the train station in Charlotte, and he was on his way toward Chattanooga, Tennessee. His journey would take him through the Appalachian Mountains and onto Chattanooga where he plans a few-weeks layover. He found a boarding house, and the folks there told him about some work that was available in the steam-engines plant; working on steam engines for trains.

The day was still young, and Thomas hightailed it over to the plant after he had put his belongings away in his room. The man told Thomas he only had a few weeks work for him because of a new business project for his company, and it would end soon. Thomas said perfect. He would take it if no experience is needed. Thomas told the man his dad worked for the Cincinnati & New Orleans Railroad in Cincinnati designing bridges that crossed over the Ohio River.

Thomas was able to visit several landmarks within the region like Ruby Falls, Lookout Mountain, and Rock City Garden. After a three-week stay, it was time to move on to the next stop which would be St. Louis, Missouri. He boarded the train westward toward St. Louis.

He was able to find a boarding house once again, but this time it took him several days to find a job that was part time. This would be a butcher helper slicing meat but of all places in an ice house. The temperature was always around forty degrees, and of course, one must wear cold weather gear to stay warm. Thomas said to himself it's a job, and he is man enough to take it on.

Thomas was there for only two weeks as he heads south toward Tulsa and Oklahoma City, Oklahoma, from there he headed south again to Dallas and Ft. Worth, Texas. As the train was rolling through the countryside of Oklahoma and Texas, Thomas was able to see many of the oil fields—each pumping oil for thirsty American cars and trucks.

Thomas wrote back home about some of the things he has seen and experienced along the way. He said that St. Louis and Dallas were very large cities, and it seems there was no end to people. He also said the people were most helpful in showing him the way to various places that he needed to go. He also said he was beginning to feel a little homesick, but he must stick with his plan.

He headed back north toward Kansas City though some of the prairie land in Oklahoma and Kansas, and the train stopped along the way in Wichita and then into Kansas City, Kansas. He left Dallas in the late afternoon and arrived in Kansas City the next afternoon around 2 p.m. and was very tired from the train ride but got up and refreshed himself a bit.

Off he goes looking for the boarding house that a fellow passenger told him about on the train ride. It was located near the stockyard and feed lots for the cattle as they are brought to market. Once at the boarding house there was no looking for a job as signs were posted everywhere "men wanted for hire." Thomas started to work feeding cows as they are brought into the feed lots. Well this was a job he knew something about from his years living on the farm. A good paying job, and he was able to save much of his money for the next adventure westward.

After Kansas City, he wants to see the fertile farm land of Iowa where much of the corn is grown. He did stop in Des Moines, Iowa, for a couple of days but no plans to stay. He was able to hook up with a gentleman that knew his way around the area to see a couple of farms. The farms were big, really big, and the farmers were very friendly and made a point to show Thomas around because he had a degree in horticulture. Thomas said he just had a desire to put his hands into the soil because of the richness of it. He said back at home most of the soil is red soil, but they are still able to grow various corps, and the soil is conducive to growing cotton.

Along the way, Thomas made sure to write to his family and keep them informed concerning his whereabouts. He traveled to many cities, and most of them he stopped long enough to work a while to build back his money supply.

When he rolled into Seattle things we're a little different as he tried to find a room in a boarding house. He arrived about nine in the morning and started to look for a room. For one thing, boarding houses where few and far between not like most cities. As the afternoon started to turn to darkness, Thomas began feel tired, and now hotels where on his list of places to stay. As he walked to each one, no one had any rooms available.

Being a good organizer when he left home the last packed item in his traveling bag was a very warm blanket that his grandmother Mayfield had made for him back when he was in his teens. Thomas knew that there was a possibility of spending the night under the stars. He now resorted to looking for a city park with a bench that he could sleep on. Well, straight in front of him a city block away was a park, but when he arrived all benches were taken by other residents.

So about 10:00 p.m., he was able to find a most comfortable sleeping quarter for the evening, but the bench was short, but by now he was just too tired to really care. Enough is enough, he was going to make it work. As he lay there trying to sleep all sorts things where running through his head. I must be clean when looking for a job tomorrow; no one will hire a person that looks like he just got out bed.

As he got up to start his day, he was sure to find a place to freshen up a bit which he did. Off he goes to look for a job, and it seemed there were a lot of jobs with posters everywhere looking for workers. He came across a large warehouse that had various produce in stock. As he started inside there stood a young lady so tall and pretty he could not believe he eyes. For Thomas he had never been one to pay much attention to girls or women. He always stayed focused on his study, work, and family.

As he was coming through the doorway of the office, he and his traveling bag got tangled up and fell. At that point Thomas was so embarrassed he could hardly get himself up as the young lady came over to help, and as she was starting to help she fell from his bag being under her feet and fell across Thomas. Well, here were both of them on the floor, and she was on top of Thomas.

Finally, the two of them managed to get off the floor and brushed themselves off when the young lady said to Thomas, "Here we are on the floor together, and I am laying on top of you, and we have never met."

By now Thomas was really embarrassed as he was trying to apologize for his action.

Her response was, "That was the most fun that I have had in a long time." So she said to Thomas, "How can we help you?"

He could hardly speak because her beauty was so breathtaking as she looked into his eyes. Well, he said, "I came in looking for a part time job so guess at this point I messed up any chance of getting one."

As they talked further, Thomas said, "I am picking up on a Southern accent."

She said that she lives in Lancaster, South Carolina, and she is in her senior year at the University of South Carolina. The young lady introduced herself as April Bennett and asked Thomas if he would like to go around the corner to a small cafe and talk. Thomas said if he could order some food as he has not eaten breakfast. When they sat down Thomas introduced himself, and he was from North Carolina near the Charlotte area lived on a large farm. He went on to tell about his college years and how he wanted to see the United States and Alaska before settling down to the farm.

April told about her grandfather inheriting this produce business from his brother about three months back, and she came out to help during the summer months. The two of them are living in her uncle's house.

Thomas said, "I just arrived last evening and could not find a boarding house nor a hotel." He said he would pay them rent if they would let him stay there while in town. His plans were to stay about three weeks and fly to Alaska.

The two of them returned to the warehouse, and Thomas met April's grandfather. He said he saw the commotion when he came in the doorway.

Thomas explained his business for being there and asked for a part time job and went on to say that he would pay him rent if he could stay at their house. He was given the job and told that he needed to talk it over his granddaughter before allowing Thomas to stay at the house. As Thomas started to work and as the day was drawing to an end, April came to Thomas and said they have a room for him, and her grandfather needed to go over some rules after he arrives. After several days had passed, both of them knew there was love in the air. They were spending all of their free time with each other and getting to know one another very well.

The day had come for Thomas to continue with his plans to visit Alaska. He called for a taxi ride to the airport. While waiting on the taxi standing outside with April, she came over close to Thomas grabbed him and kissed him like he had never been kissed before. This was the first kiss of their relationship, and boy, what a kiss for both them. As she told Thomas she was in love for first time in her life. They vowed to write to each other as often as possible as Thomas sat down inside the taxi.

Thomas arrived in Alaska for a month's stay. By this time, he had saved enough money for him to be able to spend his time just sightseeing instead of working and for his ticket back home. During his flight to Alaska, he had already composed a letter to April, and that he was missing her already. He was able to find a boarding house, and in his letter he put his address so that April could write him back. Time went by very fast, Thomas had already notified his parents about April, and he knew love was in the air for the first time.

Thomas finished out his tour of Alaska and returned home for some much needed rest. When he returned home, he found waiting for him a surprise of a life time: several letters from April that his dad handed to him at the airport. But the biggest surprise was seeing April standing in the doorway as he walked onto the porch. She had called his parents to ask permission before coming, and they agreed it would be a big surprise for him returning home. He knew for a fact that when he saw her, he was totally in love as he had missed her so very much.

Eighteen months passed, and the two were married. As a gift from Thomas's parents was a two-week honeymoon trip to the Bahama islands. They would ride the train to New York City where they would then board the cruise ship to the Bahama islands. The train would leave Charlotte at 4:00 a.m. the next morning, and it was almost a two-hour ride to the train station in Charlotte. So after the wedding and all the festivities into the evening, it did not leave much time for sleeping.

Well, what the heck who needed sleep on one's wedding night anyway. As April told Thomas's parents and her parents early that morning, she was so excited about being married and a trip to the Bahama islands she could not go to sleep, but Thomas slept like a baby.

Once again in Charlotte, Thomas IV was excited about seeing new trains since his days of working for the railroad in Cincinnati. Now the time had come for the two of them to board the train as each of them were hugging and with an occasional kiss and tears running down the faces of the three women which was Thomas's mother, April's mother, and April herself.

When the train pulled away from the station, and the two of them started to relax from all the helter-skelter of the wedding day and the preparation of getting to the train station: a nap was in order. April laid her head on Thomas's shoulder and was sound asleep in a matter of minutes.

The train was due into New York City around 6:00 p.m. They would stay one night in a hotel and then board the ship at ten o'clock the next morning. Thomas's parents had arranged a staff of people from the hotel to pick them up at the train station, take them to a recommended restaurant for an evening meal, and then have them checked into the hotel. The next morning, another staff of people took them to the cruise ship for boarding. Their parents wanted them to be pampered similar to their honeymoon at the Grove Park Inn in Asheville.

They were on their way at last with the hopes of being able to get some rest and sleep. They were on the ship for two days to reach their destination of the Bahama Islands. When the ship was pulling into the dock, it was a beautiful site to see as they could see in the distance white beaches, and the landscape all around that seem to be a paradise. Once again the hotel staff was there to greet them and take them to the hotel. The two of them were there for four wonderful days when it was time to end their stay and head back home.

They went aboard the ship to head to toward New York City. When in the middle of the night around 1:30 a.m., there were sounds of people screaming, "Fire, fire, fire!" Thomas woke up first and started telling April to get up hurry, get up fire. They were able to get to the top deck and dawn their lifejackets when they heard over the loudspeaker the voice of the captain saying, one of the cabin did catch on fire.

A fellow passenger smoking a cigar fell asleep which caught the bed covers on fire. He woke in time to notify a ship steward, and the ship's fire brigade was able to contain the fire to the one cabin and put it out. Anyone needing a drink after the scare of their life "The bar was open and good night."

After the fire aboard the ship, the two them had an uneventful trip back home to the farm. Now it was time to get down to the business of working for the farm. There are three generations living at the White Oak Farm.

Before Lily's abduction, she was still struggling with what to do about furthering her education. She wanted to be loyal to the family and go to one of the prominent universities that her family wanted her to attend. They wanted her to go into Business Law in order to take over the farm finances. Her real mission and passion in life was to be a nurse, so that she could help others. Now they just wished she was still around to talk about her desires as a nurse.

The family still believed in a miracle that Lily would be found somewhere, so that life could get back to normal, and she could once again pursue her dream in life to become a nurse.

As the family was just sitting down at the dinner table and just after the evening payer the telephone started to ring. Rachel was at home and said that she would answer thinking perhaps it was Thomas calling from Washington. The telephone carried an excited voice on the other end said to Rachel that he was Vernon Gilmore from church.

He and his wife are in Daytona Beach, Florida, on an extended business and vacation trip and wanted to report they have seen what they believe is Lily several times but they are not 100 percent sure. He described the young lady at about the same age, but most of all her bubbly personality was just like Lily's. She is working at the restaurant in the hotel where they are staying, and a man picks her up each day, but they were not sure how she arrives.

Rachel got so excited that she dropped the telephone and let out a very loud scream and everyone from the table came running in. She said to Vernon that she was sorry about dropping the telephone that she was so excited.

"Vernon," she said, "would you hold on for a minute and let me tell the others and figure out the best way to handle this so as not to scare them off."

It was decided that the Stone family would notify the local authorities, and they would notify the authorities in Daytona Beach.

"Please tell me where you are staying and a telephone number were the authorities can contact you."

She said in another telephone conversation later that they would make provisions for Thomas IV and Nancy to take a trip to Daytona Beach, but it will take a couple days for them to get there. Vernon told Rachel they would be there for another week or however long it would take to help with identifying Lily.

Thomas IV telephoned the local police and told them about the call from Mr. Vernon Gilmore and that he and Nancy would make a trip to Daytona Beach, and it will take two days to get there. It was decided that any calls to the authorities in Daytona Beach would wait until their arrival.

Thomas IV and Nancy boarded the train in Charlotte bound for Fayetteville, North Carolina, where they would then change trains with a direct trip to Daytona Beach, Florida. Excitement was in the air for all the family as the two of them got aboard the train. For the two parents, it was evident that both were nervous about what they would find in Daytona.

Was it that she went on her on freewill or was it that she was forced into going? How would she receive her parents? Will it really be Lily or someone again that resemble her and her personality? At the time of her abduction Lily was eighteen, and now she is twenty years old how will she look compared to two years ago. The man that abducted her must be the same person that took her to Florida and took the money. Will Lily know the man stole the money from the family? So many questions will need to be answered and try and sort out all of the details of the last two years. They are hoping that she will want to continue with her education.

As the two them arrived in Daytona, they headed straight to the hotel where Vernon Gilmore and his wife were staying. They checked in and immediately called Vernon and his wife Sharon. Vernon and his wife came over to their room, and they immediately called the authorities back at home, so they could contact the Daytona authorities.

As the two couples were waiting on a call from the Daytona police, Vernon brought them up to date from the last two days and said one day Lily did not show up but was back the next day, and it could have been she was off work that day. Vernon and his wife were always careful not to let Lily see them because she would remember them from church.

The telephone rang, it was the Daytona Police, and they were on their way to the hotel. Thomas pointed out to them if they were in police uniform the man holding their daughter would be spooked and would run before they had a chance to grab the guy. Thomas suggested they have plain clothes policemen come into the hotel and come to their room and discuss a strategy before moving forward. The police were cooperative and met with the Stone family and the Gilmore family.

Vernon did most of the talking because he knew more about the pattern of Lily's coming and going and as she was being picked up in the evening. The man always stayed in the dark shadows so as not to be recognized. Vernon said that he noticed that Lily always came to the hotel walking and never in the truck that picked her up at night. Could it be they are living close by? Maybe she is being dropped off a couple of blocks away?

Lily's parents wanted to see firsthand if it is truly Lily as she comes to work. The police said they would plan a strategy before they pull Lily away from her routine. They want to apprehend her abductor at the same time otherwise he would run. As the afternoon progressed, Thomas and Nancy positioned themselves in an area where they could see Lily, but it would be hard for her to see them.

Sure enough as Lily walked into the dining room, her parents knew right off that it was her, and it was all that Nancy could do to hold back from screaming and the tears. The two of them had to leave the dining room so as not to be spotted by Lily.

They had to wait until the evening when Lily would be picked up and the police would follow them to their home. The police would watch the house the next day and know when the right time would be to apprehend this guy. When the couple arrived at home, it was a very small house, and it was somewhat in an area that was all by itself. The only thing the police could do is ride by or they would detected.

The next day the police watched the house from a distance but did not see any movements from the house until it was time for Lily to go to work. The police saw the two of them come out of the house, but Lily was carrying a small child. For the police, this was going to be a problem trying to apprehend this guy. A plan would need to be put in place to separate the child from the two of them to keep the child safe.

Just as everyone suspected, he did drop Lily off one block away from the hotel. It was decided by the police they would set up a road block at the area where Lily is dropped off, so that he cannot back up or go forward, but allow enough time for Lily to get into the hotel. They would do this immediately as he starts to park to let Lily out, but they would stop other cars so as not to look like they were targeting him. The plan was presented to the parents, and they were okay with it. Because it was one block away, they decided to use a signaling system, so the authorities would know at the hotel when to pull Lily to one side, and let her know that her parents were there to greet her.

Before any of this could take place, the child had to be secure and in the arms of someone that could protect it and get the child away from any danger. The plan was in place, and now it was a matter of time until Lily would be dropped off. When the couple arrived, and Lily was on the ground, the police started to move in place one block away with the roadblock.

Several cars were ahead of him, and it appeared to the police he was nervous and might start to back up, but the police moved in quickly to prevent him from backing up. When he pulled a long side the checkpoint two policemen were there. One opens the door quickly while the other pulled the man from the vehicle. While another one on the passenger side opened the door and another policeman grab the child. Immediately the child was handed over to a female social worker to make sure the child was in safe hands and secure.

When the man was secure in the hands of the authorities, and the child was safe then it was time to signal the police in the hotel to pull Lily aside and have her parents waiting for her. Well, what a joyful moment when they all were once again united. Everyone was crying and even the police got very emotional and even more so when the child was bought into Lily.

Lily said to her parents, "Meet little Christopher, my son, we call him Chris. Where is his father?"

The police explained he is in custody of the police authorities and will be charged with kidnapping as well as other criminal charges. After the police got all the statements they needed from the family, the police left the lobby. The family met a few minutes with Vernon Gilmore and his wife Sharon to explain to Lily about them spotting her in the restaurant and they called to notify the family.

Many questions about her disappearance were needed to be asked. First question, who is this guy and what is his name? She said his name is Richard Hallman, Rick for short, and she thinks he is from Virginia. She was able to see a wanted poster for murder and armed robbery with his name and picture on it after leaving North Carolina. He did not know that she was able to see the poster.

"For the first ten months of capture, he kept me locked in a basement at an old farmhouse and repeatedly raped me. He told me many times he would kill me if I try to escape, but nevertheless, she tried but was unable to do so. At this point is where little Christopher came into being. Once he was born, Rick said it was time to leave the area and go where no one would know either of them."

The parents ask if she knew anything about the $15,000 ransom money that the family turned over to him. She wrote the letter because she was forced to, but never knew whether he received the money. She was almost sure he used the money for gambling because he did talk a lot about gambling because that was about the only thing he would talk about.

They arrived in Daytona about a month after Chris was born.

"He had enough money to pay for the rent for two months after that I had to go to work to support the three of them. During the interview for the job and starting to work Rick told me that Chris did not mean anything to him, and if she went to the authorities he would kill the baby." She said, "Regardless where Chris came from, it was a mother's instinct to protect the child."

Lily said he always carried a pistol with him even to bed, but she would have at some point gotten away from him. She experienced many times his brutal attacks on her, and she knew that he was capable of killing her or the baby or both, maybe all three of them. He was always looking over his shoulder and was ready to run at any time.

Thomas went to the train station to purchase tickets for their return home the next day. In the meantime, he called home and said they have Lily safely in their arms and would return in two days. He did not say anything about Christopher and wanted him to be a wonderful surprise to all. He called his dad in Washington about the news and asked if he could join them in two days at the farm. The authorities gave their consent for them to return home, and Rick would be sent to Virginia first for murder and then to North Carolina for kidnapping. The police informed the family he would never get out of prison for the rest of his life.

As the family was stepping off the train in Charlotte a telegram was given to Thomas IV that Richard Hallman had committed suicide in his jail cell and so ends the story of underneath the green canopy.

ABOUT THE AUTHOR

Dewey Simms was born just outside the city of Charlotte, North Carolina on a small farm. The old farmhouse had no indoor plumbing and no central heating system. Back in those days, if one would say air-condition no one would know the meaning of the words. His mother, Annie, would put large rocks in the fireplace take them out, wipe off the dust and ashes, wrap them in a cloth, and put them under the covers in the bed for warmth.

At the age of five, Dewey was blessed to have been taken in and raised by his old brother George Wesley Simms and his wonderful wife Julia Roberts Simms. After George's tour of duty of World War II was over, he married Julia, and shortly thereafter, Dewey moved in. Dewey was taught the Christian values of honesty, kindness, compassion, and hard work. He considers them Mom and Dad.

He graduated from West Mecklenburg High School in 1961 in Charlotte. Today, fifty-seven years later, the graduating class has monthly luncheons and some will travel long distances to join the luncheons.

Dewey and Alma are blessed to have two daughters: Lisa, married to Jack with two sons Blaine and Michael Lewis; Susan, married to Jeff with two daughters Alexia and Lauren Rice.

Dewey's career, a span of forty years with Charlotte Pipe & Foundry Company, Charlotte, North Carolina, brought many opportunities. There he retired as Regional Sales Manager. Charlotte Pipe and Foundry Company is a family-owned company with great values in integrity, great customer service, doing things first-class, and never having to apologize for bad services or products. He considers it a privilege to have worked there.

Having an imaginary mind, Dewey always had a desire to write a book but never had an opportunity until after retirement. In the year of 2017 and having some medical issues and was not able to move about was the perfect time to take paper and pen in hand. Not exactly paper and pen but rather an iPad and, of course, Word Document.

CPSIA information can be obtained
at www.ICGtesting.com
Printed in the USA
JSHW020959250819
1193JS00004B/49